Rev.11, M 2010

SEVEN ELEVEN

Ricky Adlam

Published by Ricky Adlam, 2024.

SEVEN ELEVEN

First edition. February 16, 2024.

ISBN: 979-8224547203

Written by Ricky Adlam.

SEVEN ELEVEN AWAY!

(INTRODUCTORY Pages 1-12)

EXT. INDIAN VILLAGE - DAY
It is several hundred years ago in India and we see a young couple leaving for their new home after their SMALL FAMILY WEDDING.
CHAN CARPENTER and WIFE RASHNA skip down the steps of a Temple dressed in white.
A CROWD of peasants tosses flower petals in the air as they move along wearing bright smiles of happiness.
HEAD PRIEST - GURU MARRISH, comes to the doorway of the white building to wave good-bye.

GURU MARRISH

Follow the path towards the end
   of the rainbow my children and
   be happy and love everything.
   Chan and Rashna stop, turn, listen, smile and run off.

EXT. COUNTRY HILLSIDE - DAY
   Chan, dressed in light blue, points over the edge of a hill out to the green valley ahead.
   Rashna stops to gather up her long white dress as she looks from a mountain cliff edge. She places her hand on Chan's shoulder and freezes, starring hard to see the house.

RASHNA

Where is our little house Chan?

CHAN

Look next to the stream, just
    follow the rainbow, right at
    the bottom. You will always
    see this from here after the
    morning rain. I built there

    for that reason. It's for you,

    my dear Rashna.
Rashna squints and then points outward.
RASHNA
Oh-my-gosh! (pause). Our house is at
the center of the rainbow. You are
a special man. I love you so much!
Rashna pulls Chan by the hand over a hill and leads him down the path towards their little dream cottage. We see
it in the distance in the valley below.

EXT. COTTAGE - NIGHT
We see a storm brew outside the BIG COTTAGE. (We See Clouds in sky and hear distant thunder)
The front door flaps open and Chan, shirt half open, steps outside to close it.
We see Rashna grab him and pull him inside. The door slams. We Hear the two giggling.
Shortly afterward it thunders and then rains.

EXT. COTTAGE - DAY
We see that it is morning. Chan opens the wooden front window. He watches as doves fly skyward.
He takes a breath of fresh air.
CHAN
It sure rained a lot but it
will stay dry on this spot.
We are much higher up on this
side of the stream my Rashna.
Chan's face disappears. (We hear tiny baby lambs crying.)
Rashna now looks out the window.
RASHNA
I see little animals caught in
the stream. Quick! Please
Chan. Go save them! Hurry.
Chan rushes outside and over to the stream where he goes into the current.
He grabs the first baby lamb, then the second, a third, and then a forth. He hands them over to Rashna.

Rashna cuddles and dries each one.

CHAN

Oh-my-gosh, there's more!

Back into the stream where the back of a drown parent passes and more baby lambs follow.

Chan picks out a fifth, sixth and then the seventh baby lamb. He sets them down and heads back to the house wet and exhausted from battling the rushing waters.

Rashna follows, as do the SEVEN BABY LAMBS into the house one by one. Chan and Rashna talk by the open front window.

CHAN (OS)

They must be from lamb flocks up

over the hill in the next valley.

So what do we do now Rashna?

RASHNA (OS)

We wait a year and then I'll make

rugs. It's a gift from above and

that will pay for clothe someday.

How many do you want, Chan my love?

The wooden window doors slam shut. We Hear them giggle.

CHAN (OS)

Seven, no eleven children Rashna.

We hear them giggle as the little lambs baa repeatedly.

CUT TO:

EXT. HOUSE - DAY

We see a small barnyard next to the house. Chan is just a bit older now. He is cutting off the wool from one of seven grown lambs. The other six lambs are shaved and waiting.

WE look through the door of the house and see TWIN BABIES in a cradle. Rashna is busy knitting a rug on a loom.

Chan walks over to the window and tosses two bags of fleece through it.

CHAN

Here you go honey. I'll be in the

garden. This one was a golden color.

Chan grabs a hoe leaning against the cottage wall and walks way smiling. He disappears into the field.

CUT TO:

EXT. COTTAGE - DAY

We see a much older Chan (mustache) exit the field and look into the cottage window. He heads over to the Sheep stool and begins to shear one of the grown up, golden haired lambs grazing outside of the house.

One of the sheep is black and it runs away in through the front door.

Now, one, two, three, four, five, six KIDS chase the black lamb outside and into the field. The three girls and four boys laugh as they run.

Chan yells out to Rashna.

CHAN

Have you finished it yet?

When do I go to market?

The cart is ready.

RASHNA

I'm almost done dear. Yes.

Your the most patient man.

Each rug is special, Chan.

Chan tosses a bag of fleece near the front door and begins

to shave the last lamb.

CHAN

Ten big rugs! Ten long years

Is a long time to wait, my love.

Rashna appears at the door and curls her front finger upward, signaling Chan to come inside in a sexy manner.

Chan stops what he's doing and goes to the door.

He tries to open it but it's locked.

He smiles and backs up.

Then Chan runs and leaps through the front window. (Pause)

CHAN (OS)

I got you-oo! Oh what a soft

rug! Mmm! Your so soft too!

Here comes baby seven.

RASHNA (OS)

Well you are certainly not!

We hear giggles. Then the six kids return and chase the seven lambs all about the yard. (Some have toy reed flutes)

The lambs baa and scatter about.

FADE TO:

INT. COTTAGE - NIGHT

We see the small fireplace and candles lit on the table.

Chan stands next to Rashna.

CHAN

The children are all asleep
up in the loft. Fast asleep!
Upside down, Chan kisses Rashna's neck and she slowly pushes him away, smiling.
Chan displays a surprised expression, leaning down from above, legs curled around the loft ladder. He flips back
onto his feet.
Rashna moves to the floor and unrolls the eleventh rug.
It is two feet larger than the other ten rugs (rolled up).
RASHNA
This is number eleven and
I just think it is now time.
Chan, I am tired of making rugs
and want to just make clothes.
Rugs will buy new shoes for all.
Chan looks at the beautiful rug and stands back.
CHAN
Rashna, I could never do this.
Your mother taught you very well.
I hate to part with any of them.
We do need much money. So, I'll
put the rugs on the cart and go
to the market, no the big city in

the morning. It will take all day.

Chan rolls up the rug. Rashna turns and takes the dirty-
dinner plates to the wash basin on the table near the
fireplace.
Above her is a cupboard where a dozen nice looking dishes and bowls are displayed. She dries each plate and places it
on a shelf. The sun is setting in the window over her shoulder. We see a green grassy hill and a beautiful, colored rainbow
that hangs in the distance blue sky.

EXT. COTTAGE - NIGHT
Chan carries five rolled rugs outside and places them on the handcart. He goes inside the cottage and exits with the
next five, placing them on top of the others on the cart.
Lastly, he carries out the seventh rug and places it carefully on top.
He moves the cart over next to the small barn and tosses a
large canvas over the top for protection.
At the cottage door Chan stops to look back at the cart. He rubs his chin, looks down and then goes inside. We hear
the two talk through the window.
CHAN (OS)
That last rug was well made.
I love the little story pictures
along the edge. What do they

tell?
RASHNA (OS)
It tells the story of Rashna and
Chan and the baby sheep and our
seven children. The story of
the elephant boy farmer and his
rug maker wife.
CHAN (OS)
Say. Put out the light. I feel
an eighth kid coming along tonight.
The light goes out and we hear the two giggling again.
FADE TO:

EXT. COTTAGE - DAY

Early morning and Chan leaves the house. He pulls the cart away across the field.
Soon he is on the hill and looking back at his cottage.
We see the house sitting at the bottom of the valley beneath a beautiful rainbow.
Chan smiles, takes a deep breath, and then moves onward.

EXT. OPEN FIELD - DAY

It is mid-day and Chan is pulling his cart.
Suddenly he looks up and stops. It has turned cloudy above. Thunder and lightning is heard.
He moves on and then stops again to look around.
The ground begins to shake.
Chan drops the cart handles and runs over to a clump of distant trees for safety.
He climbs a tree just in time as a large HERD OF ELEPHANTS
pass by on the run.
CHAN
(praying, hands up to sky)
Oh God save me. I love my wife.
I love my wife. I love my wife.
Just then, a lightning bolt strikes next to the cart and the herd stops moving. A ring of fire surrounds the cart with electric sparks. It does not burn the grass. Then the rain begins to fall.
Chan leaps down from a tree and runs over to the cart.
The elephants do nothing to harm him. The fire is gone and only smoldering smoke surrounds the cart. Rain pours down everywhere.
No rain falls on the rugs or around it as Chan moves onward.
Chan is soon through the herd and he stops to get his breath. The head elephant approaches. He rises on his back legs to salute him.
Next, the whole herd rises and bellows. They stand still a moment. Slowly, the herd moves away.
Chan moves on through the storm. Not a drop of rain lands on him or the handcart of oriental rugs. He wonders.

The big city is soon seen in the distance.

EXT. TOWN STREET - DAY

Late afternoon and we see Chan setting up to sell the rugs next to an apple cart and vegetable stand in the middle of the city

A RICHLY DRESSED MAN in white, wearing pear earrings, accompanied by TWO GUARDS wearing silk turbans, arrives.

He watches as a dirty, rag clothed, BLIND MAN stumbles into Chan's rug cart. The man falls and rises rubbing his eyes.

Chan helps him up and gives him an apple.

The blind man grabs it and looks at it and up at Chan.

He cries and then shouts, running madly away.

BLIND MAN

I can see! I can see! He has
    cured me and I can see! I can...
    The rich man moves over to Chan. He eyes the beautiful rugs, scratching his gray beard.

RICH MAN

What did you do to help him?

I must know. Tell me good man.

Chan steps back away. The two guards step forward.

CHAN

It wasn't me. It wasn't me.

It was the rugs! The rugs,

good Sir.

Quickly the man smiles and pulls out a bag of coins.

He counts the rolls and turns to Chan. His left arm is bend, crippled. He leans back on the cart, pain shoots up his arm, then he moves it all about. His eyes light up in joy.

RICH MAN

I need ten, yes ten for my gift

shop. They are finely made rugs.

Here! It's as much as a hundred

rugs would cost. I will sell

the first one to the palace

tomorrow. Stop at the shop inside

the palace gate. I live there.

Chan quickly lifts the rugs and puts five in the arms of

the first frowning guard. Suddenly he smiles and looks dumb founded and happy. Chan places the second in the arms of the other guard whose stern face turns to a grin as well.

Chan then grabs the bag of coins and bows.

The rich man looks at both guards and laughs. He removes his white turban and places on Chan's head.

RICH MAN

I've never, never seen them smile in

the eleven years they have worked

for me. Amazing! Tell me, how

many children do you have merchant?

Chan swallows hard and smiles.

CHAN

I have seven. Three, no four

boys and three girls sir. One

on the way. My name is Chan.

RICH MAN

You just bring them to my shop

and my wife will teach them all

to read and write. When they

are old enough. And ah, get

yourself some new clothes now.

The rich man winks at Chan and briskly moves down the street with the men who carry the magical rugs. (The stocky bodyguards curtsey and bow, then skip away after the Rich Man in white.)

Chan picks up the eleventh rug, places it on the cart.

He tosses the big bag of gold into the air and spins around, and around laughing deliriously.

The blind beggar passes in the other direction yelling out how he has been cured.

He stops. Kisses Chan on the cheek, then continues.

Chan catches his coin bag and tosses it high up again.

FADE OUT

EXT. COTTAGE - NIGHT

We see Chan's hand catch the gold bag by the cottage window.

Next, he tosses the bag in through the window, then the rug.

He runs around in a circle as if to leap in through the window with hands pointed outward together but stops.

Chan walks back to the handcart, grabs the bag of material off of it, then walks down over to the door and slowly enters with a cocky shake of the head. His turban tilts

to and fro.

RASHNA (OS)

Oh Chan, you kept my favorite rug.

Oh. The kids are all fast asleep.

Baby Romish is sleeping on the rug

in the knitting room with Goat-ee.

We have a quiet night for ourselves.

CHAN (OS)

How about trying for eleven kids now!

RASHNA (OS)

Seven is enough for now, but we

should always practice or we'll

forget, you rich, rich merchant man.

These coins are sure hard and smooth.

CHAN (OS)

Just like me Rashna, (pause) let's

 get to sleep now. (giggling)

Suddenly, a crash is heard from the rug weaving room.

INT. COTTAGE - NIGHT

Chan looks at Rashna and they rush into the room to check on the baby. From behind both parents, we see the goat has knocked over the bookcase and is nipping at the binding of a book on the floor.

Because the baby could be under the bookcase, they freeze in motion and listen for a noise.

Rashna holds her breath. Chan grabs her arm and points to the baby that is still asleep on the rug on the table in the next room. (Two door entry to Bed Room)

We see the kitchen table in the distance. A candle is lit on the stove. Their hands rise up to their mouths.

Rashna

But it was on the floor Chan. I

left her on the floor on the

rug. He was lying down on it.

It's a miracle!

Chan grabs her hand and shrugs his shoulders. Rashna moves to the table and takes the baby back into the bedroom. Chan rolls up the big rug and follows her.

Chan lays the rug on the floor next to the bed.

Rashna lays the baby down carefully, then hops into bed.

Chan smiles at his baby, scratches his head as he looks

over the rug, then the kitchen. Then he jumps in bed and pulls up the covers over them both.

EXT. HOUSE - EVENING

We pan about the evening sky, then we focus on the cottage bedroom window which is still lit.

We hear Chan blow out the candle, the light goes out.

We hear the two parents giggling and laughing.

Following that, we hear coins tingling about in their bed.

CHAN (OS)

Roshna. Did you move the rug?

I think the rug moved. I ah—!

RASHNA (OS)

You'd better start making the

bed move or I'm really going

to fall asleep big Chan the

Merchantman.

We hear giggling and laughing and coins tingling again.

The cameras roll upward into night sky and the stars.

FADE OUT:

RUN INTRO. CREDITS - SEE FLYING RUGS IN THE STAR LIT SKY!

(SONG SCORE: Like "HOW CAN I BE SURE", By the Young Rascals
   OR BY ROVI SHANKAR'S DAUGHTER)

(Rev 11, Jan 2010)

SEVEN ELEVEN AWAY!

INT. STORE – DAY

Present day USA

We see THREE HOODS entering a Seven Eleven Store early in the morning. The man behind the counter, ROMISH CARPENTER, looks up and quickly grabs a can of Cheese Whiz.

The largest young man pounds on the counter. The two other, clumsy teenagers push over the candy displays.

Rom pounds on the counter and whispers something in a low tone.

The big hood leans over and stares at him with a faked mad expression.

HOOD #1

What? What did you say?

The two other men rush to the counter and stare along.

Rom pulls out the can and quickly sprays their eyes.

HOODS #1 & #2 & #3

AH—-! AH—-! AH—-!

HOOD #2

I'm blind! I'm blind, you
foreign bastard. I'll get you.

HOOD #3

Take this bottle of water. Just
splash it in your eyes. Here.

The hoods pass a bottle of water around as Rom kicks them each in the ass with his foot. They hop around and slip on the spilled candy. They rise and rush out the front door.

ROM

Now get out and stay out forever!
You don't get a dime. You are the
bastards. Next time I use paint.

Looking through the front door, WE SEE the three hoods hoping away down the alley across the street as a young lady holding a loose-leaf walks up to the door.

The twenty-two year old, JENNY HART, enters and shakes her head at the sight of the candy scattered all over the floor.

JENNY

Oh-my-gosh! Did those teenage

Gangsters do this again? When
will they stop, ROM?

ROM
Oh I think it was worth the few

candies they ruined. I got them
good this time. Those hoods won't
be back for a long, long time if
they know what's good for them.

JENNY
Well, let's clean this up before
the morning crowd arrives.
Rom raises the candy stand. Both put the boxes back in place. In a few minutes all is as good as new.
ROM
So why are you here in the store,
so early my pretty American friend?
JENNY
I know it may be a lot to ask, but
I need to get some real history on
India in order to write a lesson
plan to get a job at the college.
Rom smiles. Jenny gives an innocent grin.
ROM
You just graduated from the big

University. Why do they make you
compete for a history teaching job?
Sounds silly to me Miss Jenny.

JENNY
It's an opening for a new history
course and I have to beat out all
six other college teachers. It's
for a full professorship, not an
assistant. Well, can you help me
Romish Carpenter? I'll pay you.
ROM
(starring into eyes)
Pay me? Ha! How much my young,

sweet lady? What do you have?

JENNY
Young? Your only three years

   older. Hmm. I can pay you five
   dollars an hour.

Rom turns around to think, then faces Jenny.
ROM
(leaning back on counter)
Is your boyfriend giving you the
money or your parents?
JENNY
My boy friend joined the service
last year and met another girl in
France. He just wrote me that he
got married. It was my dad, the
retired Air force pilot, who
convinced him to enlist. No, I
have a little saved for a car,
dad's graduation reward.
Rom smiles real wide now and his eyes light up.
ROM
Well I won't take any of your

   money. How about lunch for a week
   on the roof at my apartment house.
   It can be a date and history
   lesson combined. Say about –
   One O' clock today?

JENNY
(pause to think)
Oh Rom. I'm surprised!
ROM
(indignant)
Surprised? Surprised that an

   Indian boy from overseas who
   works in a dumb Seven Eleven
   store would like to get to
   know you, sweet lady.

JENNY

(hands on hips)
No! Surprised you didn't ask me

  sooner. I've hinted at least a
  dozen times.

ROM
(hands in pockets)
Ah, but before you had big muscle

  man, a man with a crew cut and
  mustang car. I only have a rusty
  old bicycle.

Jenny laughs, grabs Rom by the head, pulls it close and
whispers into his ear.
JENNY
(whispering)
You're a real special guy and I
love you a lot already. I'll
see you at one, Mister Carpenter.
She gives Rom a cheek kiss and dashes out the store.
Rom's eyes open wide.
He backs down into the counter stool.

ROM
(talking to self)
Roof. Did I say roof? It's so-so

  high. I hope I don't faint up there. (thinking) I better buy a lottery
  ticket today myself, cause things
  don't get better than this. (pause)

The girl I love likes. Not bad.
A BUSINESS MAN dressed in a suit stomps in through the door.
He grabs a paper, a pack of green gum and pulls out a ten-dollar bill.

BUSINESS MAN

So you feel luck! Ha! Well

> give me nine lottery tickets.
> Just hit any set of numbers
> you like today. See these dice,
> they ran me into a big dept.

The dice don't roll lucky

anymore!

Rom taps away for several minutes as if typing a letter.
The man takes his lotto ticket and tosses a buck at Rom.
BUSINESS MAN
Well if I win this week's super

> High lottery, I'll send you a
> share buddy. Say, what's your
> full name?

Rom holds his hand over his mouth to hide his laughter.
ROM
It is Romish Carpenter, a very
respected name in India. My
dad is a air traffic controller
in India. Good luck to us.
The man rushes out of the store, hurriedly writing the name down. At the door, he reaches in his pocket and tosses
two pair of dice back at Rom who catches them all in the air with both hands.
Rom lifts the newspaper off the counter which the business
man brought in and left. He then tosses all four dice into a waste can. He peers inside. We see a seven and an eleven
in the bottom (Angle On).
Rom walks up to the doorway.
Rom shakes his head as he places the forgotten paper back on the stack to the right of the door.
Rom then looks down at his watch, up at the wall clock, sighs, and bears a wide, dreamy grin.
CUT TO:

INT. SCHOOL OFFICE - DAY
Jenny rushes into the school hallway, then down to an office at the far end.
She knocks three times and a buzzer is heard.
She then turns the knob and enters the office.

INT. COLLEGE/OFFICE ROOM - DAY

A man in a light gray suit looks up over his glasses and rubs his thin gray hair. He points to the front center chair.
Jenny sits down nervously and smiles.

DOCTOR BALLARD leans back on his leather chair, lifts his eyeglasses off and puts them on the desk.
SECRETARY MURIEL peeks her head in by open side door, smiles and leaves.
DR. BALLARD
Muriel,(waves) I mean Jenny. Good
to see you made it here so fast.
I called your house to let you
know that the job has been narrowed
down to three girls. Your submittal
of a strong lesson plan is very,
very important in securing this
opportunity. You know that it
must be in to me by next Friday.
The desk phone rings once, stops, he looks at it briefly.
It rings again, then stops. He smiles.
He points at Jenny to continue.

JENNY

(Enthusiastic – begging)
I have an outline ready and I
have another source helping me
prepare special background data
Doctor Ballard. I will have it
all done on time. I believe that
I should be the one to teach this
wonderful class. There are many,
many students who will love Indian
History. They will, I will enrich
their knowledge and culture with
every class. And as an alumni,
I will teach the class with all
my heart and soul, sir.
Dr. Ballard places his glasses back on, looks down at the papers on his desk and then quietly speaks.
DR. BALLARD
I'll be looking forward to seeing,
what you have to offer. Don't
ask any of the others, your
former professors, for help. I
want to see what you prepare.
Good day Miss Jenny. You may

leave.

Jenny rises and quickly exits the room, closing the
door behind herself ever so quietly.
Dr. Ballard spins his chair around and peers at the window.
Shortly he sees young Jenny out the window as she skips away across the green lawn amongst the other students.
At the same time his Secretary Muriel enters and places a hand on his shoulder.

MURIEL

Talk about energy. She's quite

   promising as a candidate.

   DR. BALLARD
She's just as I was forty five
years ago. Excited and full of
knowledge and life, ready to
enlighten the world. I hope Miss
Hart gives me a decent lesson plan.
We will see Doris, we will see.
We see Jenny hop on the local bus at the corner She smiles at the driver while entering through the open door.

INT. POOL ROOM BAR - DAY
   Three hoods (Shack – Zack – Mack) exit the bathroom with paper hand towels pressed over their eyes. They plop down into three dirty chairs at the rear of the dark, unlit room. (We hear odd drinking music in the pool hall)
   HOOD #1
Well I won't fall for that one
again, bet on it, buttsey-boy.
   HOOD #2
(looking at Hood #3)
That Indian guy just won't crack,
Jack! He needs a big lesson in
payback. Right Mack?
Hood #3 leans back and falls out of his chair onto the floor. A bowl of stale popcorn falls over his head off the table.
   HOOD #3
(looking at Hood #1)
Wow! Pew! How about we get his
wife. He's married, right Shack?
Hood No.1 lowers his paper towel and smiles.
   HOOD #1
(looking at Hood #2)
He ain't married but I bet that
he's got a girl friend we can
watch for, Zack. If he's even got
a dame. If he does, then boom!
The HOODS blindly try to slap hands and fall over each other onto the floor. Pool sticks fall and they slip over them and fall down.
   They crawl over to the bar, then climb on the bar and stand up. Zack's pants are baggy and his upper ass is exposed showing a tattoo of an ashtray. (Angle On)

The bar tender, smoking a cigarette at the far end of the bar looks over and laughs at the three big goofballs.

He shines two wine glasses. He slips them in the overhead holder and walks down to take the boys orders. He peers over at stooped over Hood #2.

BARTENDER

You boys aren't old enough

    to drink. I told you before

    it's only soft drinks or pig

    piss for you or nothing.

    HOOD #2

    I think I broke my tattoo.

Shack points at the ashtray. The bar tender chuckles. Hood#1 pulls out a wallet and hands an ID card to the bartender.

    BARTENDER

    Why in hell did you get a

    Tattoo of an ashtray put

    on your creamy white ass?

    HOOD #1 & Hood #3

    (pause for laughter)

    His girlfriend liked to smoke.

    She stole his car and crashed

    it just to keep him away.

The bartender shakes his head and looks around for something to put his cigarette out in. The bar top is empty.

    BARTENDER

    (searching for ash tray)

    This is a Zoo pass. No good

    here, Shinglefits. Dam.

    HOOD #1

    I got it. Here baby cheeks.

Hood No. 1 grabs the cigarette away and puts it out on the exposed tattoo ashtray. (Really shoves it on and twists it. We hear it sizzle.).

    HOOD #2

    Yeow. I've been bitten. I'm

    dying. Help me. (Crawling about)

    HOOD #3

    I smell bacon in the air.

    (Sniffs the air)

Hood No. 3 laughs. Then bartender smacks his head in disbelief and points at Hood No. 2 as he skirts about the floor holding his butt.

    BARTENDER

    Your not dying. You pull up

    those baggy paints and get

    out of here, kid. Dis is a

    respectable joint ,Shinglefits.

The three hoods scamper away. Hood #1 pulls up Hood #2 loose baggy pants as they all move towards the entrance door.

EXT. APARTMENT ROOF - DAY

We see Rom sitting quietly on a gold, beige and red oriental carpet. It has a rainbow in the center under a rising sun.

He sets the soda cans next to the paper plates holding tuna

salad sandwiches, pickles and potato chips.

Rom looks nervously down at his watch.

We hear a boom by the door and see Jenny enter onto the rooftop wearing a smile.

She plops the loose-leaf down onto the floor and gives Rom a big hug.

Rom closes his eyes and holds on tight too long.

JENNY

Please Rom, you can let go now

sweetie. We have a lot of time

to hug later. You almost seem

  paralyzed!

The two release and sit down. Rom un-stiffens and sits.

Rom takes several deep breaths. He then relaxes.

Rom places hands next to eyes and stares only at Jenny so as not to get dizzy.

Jenny senses his fear of heights and smiles, looking into his eyes.

Each is happy to see the other.

Jenny bends over and straightens Rom's shirt collar, which calms him further.

ROM

I'm fine now. I've gotten use

  to the roof. Wow! I see you

  have your hair in a nice pony

  tail. I like that.

JENNY

Well that's good. Dad loves

  it this way too. Mom hates it.

  She just likes me to wear it

  straight and long.

Jenny sits down now, folding her legs.

ROM

Good! Then I'll get along with

your father when I meet him!

JENNY

Not unless you were in the

  Air Force because Dad only

  likes air men. He wants

me to date his Air Force

buddy's son, Brad Jetman.
Brother what a odd name.

ROM
So see him, then dump him.
JENNY
If you could help me by coming
home some time, maybe Mom would
like you and then it would be a
stand off. Mom always wins.
ROM
Gee I'm not so dizzy now. Wow!
What is this stand off. You

don't live high off the ground?

JENNY
Oh no.

ROM
Oh good.

JENNY
I got a date with him tomorrow

night to keep Dad happy. (pause)
Oh what a pretty rug and nice
lunch. Rom, you are a special
gentleman and the nicest guy

in the entire city.
ROM
I have a brother, ten years older.
He's a Doctor in New York City.

He does babies and I just do
sandwiches.

Jenny leans over against Rom.
JENNY
Oh now that's OK. You've known me

for six years. I've been trying
to get you to ask me out a long

time. You're so silly.
Jenny leans over and kisses Rom.
The rug moves. She doesn't notice.
Rom looks down.
He then shrugs his shoulders.
ROM
Oh my goodness! Hmm.
JENNY
Rom, I really want this teaching
job. I have till Thursday night

   to get my written lesson plan
   done. So let's get started. Tell
   me all about wonderful India. All

you know sweetie-pie. (pen and paper)
Rom leans over and kisses Jenny and the rug moves again.
JENNY
What was that? Boy you got some

   neat kiss. But let's get started.

Rom lifts his sandwich and takes a bite, leaning forward.
Jenny takes a bite and the mayonnaise covers her lips.
Rom then begins to speak, mouth half full and Jenny
laughs cutely. Her own mayo-white mustache wiggles.
FADE TO:

INT. HART TOWNHOUSE - EVENING
   We see Jenny's Dad, DADDY HART, in a wheelchair by the couch watching TV as the doorbell rings. He remote clicks the sound down while smirking at the news.
   Daddy Hart wheels to the door and turns the handle.
   BRAD JETSON enters and walks into the living-room.
   Jenny enters next, coming down the stairs and into the room.
   JENNY
Oh Boy! Your on time. It figures.
Well I'm ready for the movies.

BRAD

Great Jen. We'll be back by

ten sharp Mister Beck. You

can set you watch on it sir.

Dad smiles and salutes them both.

Brad salutes back and drags off Jenny though the front door. Mom enters late from the kitchen. She peeks out the front window blinds.

She watches her daughter and date walk down the sidewalk.

The two seems to walk stiffly down the block, like robots.

MOTHER HART

Dear, I have six sisters and

    know when my little girl is
in love, but it's not your
fly-boy. It must be someone
else who's very, very special.

DADDY HART

Ha! It's got to be Brad.
(Frowns)
MOTHER HART
You'd better not mess this up.
Daddy Hart rolls the wheelchair around.
He now peeks out the window.
DADDY HART
But Brad's such a hunk, a real
winner. An air force man all
the way. Just like me, honey.
And I know my little angel
loves her Daddy. It's a done

deal. I'm sure about this one.

MOTHER HART
(Folding dish towel)
She's not a airman, she's a

Graduate historian and her minds
eye is quite different. You eat
stakes and she eats vegetables.

Dad (remote) just turns about and raises the TV basketball game up louder.

EXT. MOVIE HOUSE - NIGHT
The three hoods arrive at the theater and cut in front of Jenny and Brad. Jenny looks coldly away, as does Brad.
Finally Brad turns to speak.
BRAD
Jenny I love you like a sister,
but I can't get serious cause I'm
going back to the Air Force Academy
on Saturday. Your Dad doesn't

know. I'm getting more training.

Jenny smiles and hugs Brad.
JENNY
Oh thank God, cause I love my
new boyfriend Rom Carpenter.
Oh what a relief Bradford.

Brad laughs.
The three hoods suddenly turn about and pound their fists.
Jenny jumps back holding her hand over her mouth.
HOOD #1
So you're Rom's new girlfriend.

 That's just too bad for you now.

JENNY
Brad! Those three wrecked Rom's
store today. Run, quick. Run.
They beat up kids all the time.
Jenny trips over a sidewalk brick and falls down onto her bottom. Brad just shakes his head at the three goofballs.
Hood #1 hits Brad in the face but he doesn't even flinch.
The hood falls back in pain but rebounds back to his feet and takes a fighting stance.
Brad smirks, then proceeds to pound each man with several lightning fast blows to the stomach.
They swing fists but only glance Brad. He's moves fast.
Brad pushes them over onto each other.
Then Brad extends his arm out to Jenny. She rises and steps on each Hood's hand as she passes by.
Jenny grabs his arm and laughs at the three Hoods lying on the sidewalk. (Sticks out her tongue at them all)
Brad grabs their tickets, gives one to a late arriving old couple who smile back great-fully.
Brad and Jenny enter the movie theater arm in arm.
CUT TO:
INT. SEVEN ELEVEN STORE - DAY
Morning and Rom is clearing the center glass doors with a towel and spray when Jenny arrives.
Rom steps back to let Jenny enter. She kisses him on the cheek.
JENNY
Good news. Brad is going to

 Air Force School. I want you
 to stop by my house tonight.

We can go to a movie or to
the zoo and see the Indian

 elephants. Later we can go
 up onto the roof, sit on the
 rug and count the stars.

ROM
Well, do I get to say anything

 About this my fast talking
 girlfriend? Can we watch somewhere
 lower than the roof?

JENNY
No! I have to type up yesterdays
notes that you gave me. I can't
do two lunches in a row but

tonight I'll be free. The weather
is clear, no clouds and no fear
of heights my sweet brave man.

Jenny and Rom kiss for at least a minute.
He shakes his head, yes. She kisses his forehead.
JENNY
Make it seven, that's after

Dad has eaten. See you then.
The white house three blocks
down.

Out the door she scoots, leaving Rom with a wide grin.
Rom sprays the door to clean it as he watches Jenny. She rushes down the sidewalk towards her home, a big townhouse.
As Rom sighs, then the hoods rush around a corner towards his store. Rom looks up just as the three rush inside.
Rom quickly sprays them in the eyes again but with the Windex cleaner and cheese whiz. He does not hesitate.
All three hoods turn and stumble out the door. Rom boots them each in the ass as they stagger away.
ROM
And don't come back. I told
you jerks not to come in here.
Someday I'll own my own Indian

Rug store and never have to
deal with such stupid hoods.
Let them rob the rich kids
Back at school. Allah, Jehovah,
God, please hit them with a
big red truck today.

Rom spits by the front door and heads back in side the Seven Eleven store.
FADE TO:
INT. HART TOWNHOUSE - NIGHT
We see Jenny looking out the front door window for Rom.
She looks dressed to kill tonight in a tight, red jumper.
Dad wheels into the hallway, out from the kitchen. His hands are black with grease from fixing an old lawn mower out back.
DADDY HART
My! My sweet angel girl sure looks

pretty tonight. We hardly have any
grass to mow and the mower breaks
down. What luck.

JENNY
Daddy, Tommy gave your mower to
Peter Piscatello and he borrowed
his to fix for him. It's not
our mower you fixed. Do you

remember now?

DADDY HART
Oh yeah! The two are cutting

lawns this summer. I forgot!
(pause) Hey! How was the date

with Brad? (hands behind head)
Mother Hart comes down the stairs and gives Dad a hard look. She silently heads down the hall to the kitchen.
JENNY
It was fine. I have someone to
meet tonight. You'll like him.

He's special, sweet, brave and
very kind. He's—-

The doorbell rings.
The door opens and Rom is pulled inside.
He is a little off balance.
JENNY
This is Romish Carpenter and I
love him dearly Daddy. Rom is
helping me get the big job.
Dad looks him over and squints, frowns.
DADDY HART
Can you fix a lawn mower? Hey,
do you fly boy? Fly any boy?
ROM
No and no, but I'll gladly try
to help the Dad of my Jenny.
Someday I'll own a rug shop and
then I'll—-.
Dad wheels away down the hall to the basement door.
Mother Hart returns and stands just behind him with hands folded.

DADDY HART

You can date my daughter all you

want, but I won't consent to

any marriage boy, unless I see

you fly.

ROM

(smiling)

See you later, Mister Beck?

DADDY HART

(loudly)

When you fly, boy. Fat chance.

Dad heads out the back door ramp, then down the basement.

We hear him laughing profusely out back.

Mother Hart enters and rushes over to shake Rom's hands.

She hugs (frowning) Rom, his feet rise off the floor.

MOTHER HART

If my Jenny loves you, you must

be very special. It's what's

inside, not how rich your are or

where your from or how much hair

you have or if you fly airplanes.

(long look over stare)

My husband was an Air Force pilot

and wants to ride in a jet before

he dies. Let Jens Cousin Nicky

marry an Air Force pilot. Now

go out and have some fun. Get.

Rom smiles and the two exit through the front door.

Mother turns and heads back to the kitchen ramp - basement door. She grins as she closes it. She then locks the door. Then she heads upstairs.

Soon Daddy Hart is heard knocking at the basement back door, yelling to get let in.

Upstairs we see Mother Hart close her bedroom door and turn up the radio loud. She smiles as she makes the bed.

Dad keeps on pounding on the locked basement door (looking mad).

EXT. ZOO - NIGHT

Jenny and Rom stroll into the zoo. We See them head over to visit the Indian elephants exhibition. (Following shots)

They move up to the fence, hand in hand.

JENNY

I once rode a paper elephant

when I was eleven in the town

spring parade. When do the

elephants go inside?

ROM
They stay out till nine in

summer. Then the lights go out.

Suddenly <u>THREE (3) ELEPHANTS</u> move over to Rom. Their trunks rub his head.
JENNY
Wow! They love you Rom (pause)
If only Dad could love you too.
He won't let me engage or marry
anyone who doesn't fly. It's
that Air Force thing.
Rom pets the elephant's trunks. Jenny joins him.
In the distance we see Doctor Ballard and wife sitting by
a food stand sipping a coke through two straws.
He lowers his glasses and looks at Rom and Jenny in the distance.
He taps his wife arm and points. They watch them petting.
DR. BALLARD
Oh now I see. She's in love
with history and live culture.
Jenny Hart's lesson plan should
be quite enlightening, indeed.
DR. Ballard and wife watch with half a smile.
A MOTHER WITH TWO DAUGHTERS arrive at the railing and watch the elephants briefly. One girl has a cast on her leg.

Her seven year old is in a wheel chair. She covers her face whenever her mom tries to take a picture. The other sister, eleven, leans over but gets pushed away. They both wear blue shirts, one with a red seven and the other with a red eleven on front and back.

GIRL 7

Not in this chair or the kids
    will tease me. No, No, No!

Rom looks at Jenny and winks. He walks over to her wheel chair and smacks her knee (on the cast).

ROM

So you broke your leg. I

don't mind you using my

back as a stool.

Rom kneels down two steps from the chair on hands and knees.

The little girl smiles and rises up. She hops over and sits on his back. She pushes wheelchair away out of the picture.

(We hear the radio the older sister is holding is playing LIKE A RED RUBBER BALL by THE CIRCLE.)

Mom takes several flash shots and smiles.

A crowd of twenty arrives behind mom and claps. Soon everyone is kneeling and taking pictures the same way.

In the distance we see Dr. Ballard and wife laugh.

As Rom and Jenny leave the area, Jenny gives Rom a big hug.

WE SEE Dr. Ballard and wife laugh do the same using a passer by to take a picture.

Next, Ron and Jenny turn and view the small monkeys in through their cage. They see two monkeys, one kneeling and the other sits on its back. This sight makes them laugh.

Rom and Jenny exit the park in the same direction that they entered. Jenny looks back to see every ZOO CROWD family kneeling and sitting, taking pictures everywhere.

Jenny and Rom laugh as they walk away down a zoo path, hand in hand.

JENNY

My dad retired from the service.

He works as a vet consultant at

the Zoo. That's just why I never

go there. Maybe I will go now.

Rom shakes his head, understanding her statement.

We see people kneeling here and there and sitting for pictures by different animal cages and laughing at their positions.

In the distance the three Hoods enter the zoo grounds and point at ROM and Jenny.

HOOD #1

Stay back so he don't spot us.

Head over to the monkey cage,

  boys. Keep an eye on them.

They walk over to the monkey cage. Hood #2 looks inside and reaches through the bars. A monkey grabs his earring and hair and rams his head against the bars a dozen times, then lets go. (Thud –thud –thud –etc)

Hood #3 looks on. Hood #1 doesn't see a thing.

HOOD #2

Oh my God. I think he tore out

my brains. You bad, bad monkey.

He falls down to the ground. (We see a number of bumps on his scalp) Hood #3 rushes to the bars to yell at the monkey. He points at the little animal and shakes a fist.

HOOD #3

Why don't you pick on me, you

little hairy meatball. What do

You say to that?

The monkey pisses on his shirt. Hood #3 turns around and has a bright yellow (ten inch wide) stripe up and down his white shirt. He walks over to Hood #1.

HOOD #1

What did you do? You smell.

HOOD #3

That hairy animal pissed all

over my new shirt. I think

the zoo is an awful place.

Hood #1, Hood#2 and Hood #3 turn toward the cage to yell at the monkey and an ape appears and thumps his chest.

HOODS # 1-2-3

Oh Shitaroonie!

Seeing the mad ape, the three Hoods frantically run off and out of the zoo. Hood #3 holds his nose and Hood #2 holds his head as they run.

EXT. HIGH SCHOOL – LATE AFTERNOON

Hood no. 1, dressed in black leather, grabs two teen young boys outside the High School in an alley.

The small boys punch at the teen. He just laughs at them when they are done. Then the two reach into their pockets and pay up.

The two twelve year olds shake in fear.

Hood 2 and Hood 3 arrive from the far end watching the bigger thug count his money.

One of the hoods kicks a garbage can for attention.

The Hoods look, laugh and pound their fists into a car door (Old Pickup near by). They stop to make muscles at each other.

Hood 1 waives at some kids to come on closer.

They run away. Six other kids see them and run the opposite way.

The three Hoods laugh and prance back down the alley.

EXT. STREET - NIGHT

WE hear a lot of moaning, punching and kicking of trash cans.

After a few quiet moments, the three hoods walk out from behind three cars. Two young men in torn suits run off in fear. One man is missing his trousers, the other no shoes.

We see the three Hoods counting money, smiling, walking.

One hood carries the suit pants over his shoulder.

The other has the leather vest on and the third has a pair of shoes tied and hanging from his belt.

We glance back into the alley and see a third young suited salesman, hanging upside down from a fire stairway ladder. His feet are tied to the lower rail.

A close up shows his bloody open mouth gasping for air.

His hands dangle about in the air, eyes in shock.

His blue underwear is marked on the ass with the words:

Tougfh! Shitzie! (Angle On)

(FOLLOWING)

We watch the three Hoods walk away down the street. They stop by a street light a block down to talk.

HOOD NO.1

Leather boy back there thinks

  he's tough. These are nice
  leather pants he had.

HOOD NO.2

Maybe we ought to go back and

borrow his undies and socks too.

HOOD NO.3

I got his wallet and you know

something guys?

The other two look up at Hood No.3 and snarl.

HOOD NO.1 and NO.2

What pea brain.

Hood No. three waves the wallet in the air.

HOOD NO.3

It ain't leather, it's vinyl.

  Leather boy was using vinyl.
  Ha! Ha! Ha! Ha! (farts)

They all laugh at each other hysterically.

FADE TO:

EXT. APARTMENT ROOF - NIGHT

The roof door opens and Rom drags Jenny by the hand over to his old oriental, rainbow colored rug. They flop down. Both laugh for a moment.

Rom turns over onto his back and then so does Jenny.

Both then stare up at the stars. (Angle On stars)

ROM

Oh! Those Zoo people were nice.

Look! The stars are so beautiful

tonight, Jenny my love.

JENNEY
Yes they are. It was you that made
the little girl happy and everyone
else too. Oh! Rom, you called
me your love! Boy it took long to...
Rom turns over and kisses Jenny on the cheek. The rug moves over a foot and Jenny's eyes open wide.
It glows a moment in the sunlight but neither notices.
JENNY
What was that? The building?
Maybe nothing.
Rom smiles.
He sighs.
He rolls onto his back again.
ROM

Who knows. You know when I was a

boy of seven I was out on a picnic
with my Grandfather Yusuf and we
sat on this very rug. He left
to get water from the stream and
an unseen heard of elephants came
rushing out of nowhere. Maybe to
get away from a lion. I don't know.
Jenny rises up on her elbows. She stares attentively at Rom.
JENNY
Yes. Yes. Go on Rom. Go on.
ROM
They went around me and never
touched the rug. Then ...
JENNY
What else?
ROM
I was thinking of buying a gun.
I want to teach those Hoods that
keep threatening me a lesson. I
am the runt of the litter in my
family and I don't have my big
brother to protect me. I get
anxious leaving the store alone.
JENNY
Oh Rom. Your such a gentle man.
Don't let them change you. Stay

away from guns, please. For me.

Rom shakes his head in agreement and then yawns.
He stands and walks to the roof edge.
Rom looks out over the roof, quivers like he is dizzy, then
looks down into his lap.
He starts to sway off balance. Jenny puts a hand to her mouth.
Rom takes a deep breath and calms down. He backs away.
Plop he falls down on the rug next to Jenny.
ROM
You know I only get dizzy when

I'm up high. On a three foot
ladder I feel faint. I'm not sure
why this happens, Jenny.

JENNY
So what else about this nice family

rug of yours?

Rom continues with his story.
ROM
A half a year later, after the

Elephant thing happened, I fell

asleep on this rug at my dear
Grandfather's old wooden house.
It had seven rooms and a very big
living room. My Grandma was gone
shopping, you see Jenny. So, so
the house caught fire with me, me
in it. The fire brigade saw me
asleep inside but couldn't get to
me. It was much too hot and too
dangerous. The fiery roof was

caving in when my Grandfather
arrived home. He was then at odds.

The others restrained him outside.
Rom looks Jenny deep in the eyes.
Both stare motionless.

(We hear tense romantic music in the background)
FADE TO:

EXT. HOUSE - NIGHT
We briefly see the burning house, GRANDPA YUSUF outside, little Rom sleeping on the rug and twenty frightened VILLAGERS. The carpet carries Rom out the broken front window to the grass hill. (FLASHBACKS as they talk.)
FADE BACK TO:

EXT. APARTMENT ROOF – NIGHT
We are back on the roof with Rom and Jenny.
ROM
I woke up briefly and saw Grandpa
but the hot fumes put me back to
sleep. He stood there with tears
in his eyes and prayed to God and
the stars. Then, so the villagers
tell me, the rug rose and flew me
safely out the window, lowering me
gently on the soft grass of the
cow pasture many, many yards away.
Jenny smiles, but tears roll down her cheeks.
JENNY
Then what happened Romish?
ROM
(looking into her eyes)
Then my Grandfather rushed over
to me and woke me up. I thought
it was a dream. I saw the burning
house and cried on his shoulders.
I still think it was a dream.
Rom takes a big gulp.
ROM
I asked Grandpa what happened and
he told me. Then I asked him
if he thought the carpet could fly
again. Yusuf told me...
JENNY
Yes! What? What? What?
ROM
That it will only fly for, for

true love. I don't understand.

I know he loved me a lot. A few
years later he died in his new
home and he left me the old rug.
It helps remind me of him, Jen.
So, I did once flew, but not
on a plane. Do you believe it?
Jenny hugs Rom tight and kisses him again.
JENNY
I will tell this story to my class.
I won't mention you, but I'm going
to put it at the end of my lesson
plan. Now I know I'll get the
teaching job at the university. I
felt you were special, you are.
Rom scratches his head and leans back on his elbows.
Jenny points to the sky at a shooting star.
Rom nods his head.
ROM
What? Oh I see.
He points now.
JENNY
I know deep in my heart that
someday you'll get that rug
store cause your such a nice,
wonderful guy.
ROM
I hope so. Maybe I'll call it,
The Village. That sounds nice.
Jenny kisses Rom. She holds it for a long, long time.
CUT TO:

EXT. BAR - NIGHT
We see the three (3) Hoods enter a local bar and shortly after get tossed back into the street by TWO BOUNCERS in pink leather and the BARTENDER who's wearing a white smock. The smock reads, Gay Harry's in bold letters.

BARTENDER

(Loud gay voice)
    I don't care who's Uncle your

    related to, I'm not paying
    a dam cent for protection.

    Get your three little queer

    asses off my street.

The bartender follows the two other men back into the bar.
After a brief moment, the three (3) Hoods rise up off the street and brush themselves clean.
Then, the leader pulls out three brass knuckles. He gives one to each HOOD. All three smile, then pound their hands.
Hood No.3 makes an expression of pain for a moment.
The three re-enter the bar and we hear a lot of glass smashing and chairs smashing. (Lights flashing)
A moment passes and then we hear a cash register ring.
The gay bouncers walk out and pause, then collapse to the sidewalk.
Out come the three (3) Hoods, each is counting a wad of money. They are bleeding (scratches) but seem happy.
HOOD NO.3
Hey boys?
HOOD NO.1 and NO.2
What cucumber brain.
He pauses and they stop.
HOOD NO.3
The bartender has a vinyl wallet
too! Maybe old leather boy's

    his son.

All three (3) Hoods laugh hysterically.
FADE TO:

EXT. SEVEN ELEVEN STORE - DAY
Late morning - six schoolboys wait eagerly for (yawning) Rom to open the store so they can purchase one of his super cheap, super stuffed submarine hero sandwiches for lunch later at noon.
The door opens and they all rush in single file, grab a soda can and sub from the freezer,
then pick up a candy bar,
then slap two dollars each on the counter
and then rush out of the store to school.

ROM

Sorry boys. I was up late last

night. Someday you may just

understand. Be good at school.

Rom heads back into the store room where he spots a broken upper window, a high set one meant only for day light.

He just shakes his head and heads to the front counter.

As Rom comes out, the three Hoods enter and stand by the door.

All three wear small bandages of some kind here and there on their heads and arms.

HOOD #1

Are you gonna pay up and be

a smart guy.

HOOD #2

You better pay up if you know

what's good for your girlfriend,

nut brain.

HOOD #3

Yeah! Yeah! Nut brain. Owe!

Rom grabs a broom and heads for the three who rush out of the store like scared rabbits.

Rom swings the broom around in mid air (cursing under his breath).

He opens the door to yell out at the scampering juveniles.

ROM

Please come back so I can

thrash you all about, you

dumb cucumbers.

Several customers walk up and enter to pick up newspapers. They laugh as they read about the lucky man who won the lottery. (We see the back of a man holding up a ticket.)

Rom glances at the headlines as he heads behind the counter. He puts down the broom and smiles at each customer as they place money on the counter and leave the store.

(The Producers cameo in this film)

LAST CUSTOMER

Looks like someone has won the big
    lottery at last. It took seven
    long months until it ended on

    July eleventh. He says it was
    his seventh ticket and the
    eleventh time he bought them.

    Boom. The man briskly exits the store.
    Rom just shoves the money in the register and smiles.

INT. UNIVERSITY - DAY

We see Jenny rush down a hall past the wooden door labeled DR. Ballard to the next door. She opens the glass door and enters, holding her final teaching plan submittal to her chest.

We see the secretary at the desk. She waves her to come inside, with an outstretched hand.

The wooden door closes behind Jenny.

INT. OFFICE - DAY

Jenny hands the completed lesson plan to Secretary Muriel.

Muriel gives the papers a glance, gives Jenny the crossed fingers sign. Jenny then enters through the side rear door to Dr. Ballard's office.

Muriel returns and waves Jenny to leave.

She stands silent and gives Jenny a long hard stare.

Jenny finally gets the message and dashes out the door.

Muriel smiles and sits back down in her chair just as the phone rings. She leans back and lets it ring away, fingers crossed up in the air.

INT. HART TOWNHOUSE - DAY

We see Rom standing outside the front glass door.

Mother Beck opens it and lets him inside.

Rom has a set of tools in his hands.

He looks closely at his wristwatch.

MOTHER BECK

Jenny won't be home for lunch

today. Oh you're here to meet
the repair challenge. You must
love my Jenny very much. Go

down the hall, the basement door
is to the right Rom. Good luck.
(Following Shots of Rom through the Beck's house)
BROTHER TOMMY is standing in the kitchen with hands in his pocket. He follows Rom to the door and down the kitchen steps to see what Rom is up to in the basement that leads out to the back yard.

Rom spots the old lawnmower and begins to look it over, turning a screw with his screw driver, then yanking the pull string.

Tommy sits down on the third step and chuckles.
Rom checks the oil and then the gas, pulls the string a dozen times. He then throws his hands up in the air.
TOMMY
So what are you trying to do?
It's not even your machine, bud.
Rom sits on a stool, tosses the screwdriver into his tool-box in frustration.
ROM
Well young man, I was trying to
fix the machine to impress your
father for Jenny. But I guess
this idea is not going to work
this day. I've never fixed one

before.

Tommy laughs and walks over to the machine.
Rom hands tools over to Tommy.
Tommy hands him back a lump of chewed chewing gum.
TOMMY
Shoot. The only darn thing wrong
with it is the spark plug. It's
cracked. It was stuck but I
got it off last night. I'll
screw it back on. You owe me

one now, -—Bud.

Tommy smiles, grabs a tool, reaches down and turns the plug.
In a few seconds the mower is fixed.
ROM
Thank you brother Tommy.
Rom yanks on the start chord twice.
A loud hum rings out as the mower turns on.
A few moments later, Rom turns off the machine.

Tommy stands and smiles.
Rom wiggles his eyebrows and slaps hands with Tommy.
He grabs his toolbox and they head back up the steps.
TOMMY
That should put you in solid

 with my Dad. Now all you got
 to do is learn to fly. Ha.

 ROM
I surely would take lessons but
I am afraid of heights. I get

 dizzy.

 TOMMY
 Gee that's too bad. I like you.

Tommy pats Rom on the back.
He takes his chewing gum back and pops it into his mouth.

 ROM

Even as a boy, I only rode the
small baby elephants. Someday
I may get over this fear I hope.
I came to USA on a boat. I'm
OK if I don't look down.
Tommy stops at the top of the steps.
TOMMY
Do you have another brother?
ROM
Yes. He took all the brains.
He's a big shot baby doctor in

 New York.

Tommy rubs his chin and smiles.
TOMMY
I'll have to meet him sometime.
ROM
Where is Mister Hart today?
They sit down at the kitchen table.
TOMMY
Oh he's a Zoo vet. He directs

all the pet handlers at the Zoo.
His flying days are over since
the family plane crashed.

Rom's eyes light up.
ROM
I heard he was hurt. How long

ago?

TOMMY
Ten years and they say it's
a permanent injury to his spine.

Tommy and Rom rise. They enter the hallway and head for the front door.
Mother Hart enters the kitchen and looks at a wall picture of her and hubby standing and waving at Niagara Falls.
(Angle On)
Boom! We hear the front door slam. Soon Tommy is back in the kitchen with mother Hart.
MOTHER HART
How do you like Jenny's new
boyfriend?
TOMMY
Seems like a nice guy! I can
see them together. He is low
keyed like Jenny.
MOTHER HART
You better return the mower
and bring back your fathers.
Tommy opens the cabinet door and grabs a cookie.
TOMMY
The contract to cut the hotel
grass ends this weekend. I'll
switch mowers tomorrow. Rom

might give me a job now. He
owes me a favor.

Mother Hart opens the fridge, pulls out a read-made sandwich.
Tommy takes the sandwich.
MOTHER HART
I knew you'd rush away without a
proper lunch so I made you your
favorite, peanut butter and jelly
(pause) with bananas. Now skidoo!
Tommy stuffs his mouth with one large bite, hugs mother and exits out the back door acting goofy and stupid like.

Mother Hart shakes her head at the sight of her silly son.

INT. SEVEN ELEVEN STORE - DAY

We see Jenny enter the store and walk around looking for Rom.

A thin TEENAGE BOY, WAYNE, in blue jeans comes out of the back and stands behind the counter.

A few minutes later a YOUNG TEENAGE GIRL comes out of the back, Katie.

She straightens her hair and tucks her blouse into her skirt.

JENNEY

Is Rom around anywhere?

KATIE

Oh he'll be back. He went to
    repair something, somewhere.

WAYNE

Yeah! You'll have to wait! I've
    seen you here before, right?
    The girl walks over to the boy and elbows him in the ribs.
    Jenny laughs and sits down on the paper stand.
    Jenny picks up the paper and starts to read it!
    TEEN BOY
    You going to pay for that girl?
    The teen girl elbows him again.
    KATIE
    Don't mind him, when he was

      born the doctors dropped him
      in a tub of LSD. He thinks he
      owns the store. You can read
      all you want until Rom returns.

    Jenny smiles at the young girl.
    Just then the tall man in a suit from the day before enters the store.
    He walks over.
    SUITED MAN
    I was here a day ago. Where is
    the other guy, the one with dark
    hair and sense of humor? I,
    I need to find him. I've got
    something for him. Can anyone
    tell me?
    Jenny straightens a white bandanna on her forehead.
    JENNY
    I'm waiting for him myself.
    He runs the store and should
    return sometime soon.
    SUITED MAN
    Well I can't wait long so I'll
    have to return. Tell him the
    seven eleven man from the other
    day was asking for him. OK?
    The teenagers shake their heads as he exits the store.
    The phone rings.
    The girl picks it up immediately.
    KATIE
    Yes! I take orders. Ten subs with
    no onions or peppers. Great. Yes

we deliver. Yes. Where? Sodas.

Yes! Yes! Yes!

The girl grabs ten subs out of a box and two six packs. She then tosses them into an empty box.

The teenage boy walks next to her and rubs her thigh. He gets a finger flick to the head. He backs up, holding his head.

WAYNE

Those don't have peppers now?

KATIE

We add them, now don't we? Here.

deliver this down the block at

the travel agency. Move out

bone brain and don't return till

tomorrow. Book a flight to the

moon.

The boy grabs the box and raises it to his shoulder.

WAYNE

(Like Arnold S.)

I'll be back! Baaaby!

He exits the store. Both girls laugh.

JENNY

How did you meet him? He seems

like he's a real tease.

KATIE

Sometimes he is but he has a serious

side as well. If he didn't I'd

never have taken this job here.

JENNY

Say. How do you like working

for Romish? Is he a good boss?

Jenny leans on a display.

The teen stops to think a moment then replies.

KATIE

Well, he's always clean. He wears

a lot of cologne too. They're

always all done when I get here.

JENNEY

The subs?

She points to the side fridge holding the sub sandwiches.

KATIE

Yeah, at the last store I worked

they made you come in early to

prepare a few dozen quick picks.
Rom always has them ready to go
in four separate boxes. He knows
his business alright. I wouldn't

  work for anyone else.

JENNY
Well that's nice to know cause
he's my boyfriend. That's good.
A moment later Rom enters the store and greets everyone.
ROM
Ah Ha! Good afternoon my friends.
So how are things going today? I
guess the run on subs has started.
KATIE
Yep! Odd-ball is out delivering.
We must have sold forty-five subs

  between twelve and one. Six left.

Rom and Jenny hug, then he heads behind the counter, plops
two subs into a bag with two bottles of Snapple and heads out to the front door. Rom grabs Jenny's hand as he leaves.
ROM
Watch the store and I'll return.
We have a history lesson to do
so I'm taking a late lunch.

KATIE
Sure boss. You take your time.
I'll watch everything. I don't
have art class today.
Jenny waves bye-bye as Rom pulls her out of the store.
We See the two skip across the street and down through the alley, heading for the apartment house roof above the
seventh floor roof.
The teenage girl heads into the back room and turns the radio up loud. (Hear song THE LADY IS A TRAMP by
Ricky Pitt)
She knocks over a jar of pens and pencils to the floor. She bends over to pick them up off the floor.
A moment later, Tommy Beck enters the store to return a screwdriver that was left in the basement.
He walks over to the counter but no ones there, so he walks to the side room where the music is coming from.

INT. STORE ROOM - DAY

Tommy enters the back office room and sees the Teenage Girl bending over to pick up the last few pens.

He reaches down over her stooped body to help grab the last pen. She holds his arm and looks up.

She grabs his arm and pulls it hard, to make him fall a little off balance.

She rises tossing the last pens onto the desk and reaches back to the left to grab his other arm.

Tommy rises as she does. He's quite surprised when his arms and hands are snuggled into place around the girl's waist.

KATIE

Well you took long enough. So

you delivered the subs?

TOMMY

I'll deliver anything you want.

The girl reaches back to feel Tommy's arm muscles. She then realizes it is not her goofy boyfriend stopping over her.

KATIE

Hey wait. I thought you were

someone else. Who are you?

She spins around in Tommy's arms and freezes.

The two lock eyes.

Suddenly, she grabs both shirt collars and pulls his face up to hers.

She runs her eyes all over Tommy's face and then kisses him.

They stop kissing. Both blush.

They disengage briefly. Tommy places a tight hold around

her waist and kisses her quickly once more on the nose.

The two slowly spin around the office as the music plays, locked in a hug with their minds in the clouds.

The song finally ends and the two slowly separate to talk.

(We Hear song ON A CLEAR DAY by Ricky Pitt}

She takes a second to gather back her strength. She breaths deeply.

KATIE

(whispers)

Ahhhhh! So who are -—yah?

TOMMY

I'm a friend of Roms. Just

returning a tool.

Tommy reaches into his back pocket and pulls out the tool.

TOMMY

See. I'll leave it on the counter.

The teenage girl smiles sexy like.

KATIE

I ah, thought you were my

ah, former boyfriend. He's

out delivering some subs.
TOMMY
Oh I see. He's just a friend?
KATIE
No we just hang around. I
have all study hall Fridays.
What about you?
TOMMY
Two study halls, one after lunch
and one before. So if you don't
have to check in, you must be a
senior too. Well that's perfect.
KATIE
Oh you can say that again.
She leans against the desk and grabs the edges, glancing up
into Tommy's eyes.
He moves closer as he slips the tool into his back pocket.
She wets her lips with her tongue slightly. Smiles. Bats eyes.
TOMMY
Movies tonight?
She silently nods.
TOMMY
Oh! My names Tommy and I'll
be back here at seven sharp.
Tommy rubs his nose against her nose. He leaves the room, heading out to the front. She sighs.

INT. STORE - DAY
We see Tommy move around the central register counter, then towards the front door.
Just as Tommy exits, the delivery boy enters, looks around a moment and walks behind the counter.
We see the teenage boy ring up the register and place the sub money inside. He slams the drawer shut. He then turns to look for his female partner.
WAYNE
Yooh! I'm back pretty baby. I
got a ten buck tip this time.
They were really nice today.
Where are -—you?
He turns to enter the back room with arms stretched out.
A wet towel comes flying out and lands on his head.
He trips over a box, gets his foot caught in the mop pail which has wheels, then spins out of control towards the front candy rack trying to get his balance.
Finally he falls down against the candy rack and everything spills all over onto him.

The Teenage Girl enters and stands by the counter.
She looks down at her clumsy partner and shakes her head in disgust.
KATIE
You know! You are a little bit
like goofy. I have to leave now
to get my hair done today. I—-
ah! I have choir practice later.
OK?
The Teen Boy looks up, she smiles, he smiles.
A few more bags of M&Ms fall down on his forehead.
He tries to rise but then falls back down on his back.
She grabs her bag and dashes out of the store.

EXT. ROOF TOP - DAY
Rom and Jenny arrive and head over to their usual spot.
They sit on the rug by the alley side of the building.
Rom opens the bag and tosses a sub sandwich to Jenny.
He removes his sub and then places the bottle of Snapple down along side on the rug in front of himself.
Jenny makes a drinking jester and so Rom winds up and slowly pitches her bottle into the air.
Jenny fumbles around and it lands on the roof top wall,
the bottle starts to roll away on the ledge.
Jenny rises.
Rom quickly springs ahead of her and snatches the bottle up,
leaning back over the edge.
JENNY
Wow-We! That sure was close, Rom.
ROM
Oh yes Jen, it was too close. Oh
boy! Oh boy, I'm dizzy now.
Rom looks down into the alley and sways.
Jenny moves closer to steady him as he turns away, struggling.
Rom quickly sits himself down.
JENNY
Well what was that?
Rom catches his breath and then smiles, sitting up, leaning back on his hands.
Jenny looks over the edge and then stands beside Rom.
ROM
Oh I am used to it. -—I'm afraid
of heights. I wasn't always. It
started when I was eleven. About
four years after the fire at dear
Grandpas house. I can't re- re-re-
remember what happened.

JENNY
What do you remember, Rom?
Rom grabs his chin and thinks.
ROM
I chased a fox into the forest.
He tried to eat, ha, my neighbors
chickens. That afternoon I returned
with a headache, a bump on my head
and from that day to this I can
not stand high places.
Jenny rubs his scalp and he calms down.
She continues to rub his scalp with two hands.
ROM
Ah! That feels good. That is
just heaven. Ah! Ah—-!
Standing behind Rom, she continues and rubs his scalp.
He acts like he's in heaven. (eyes roll about)

JENNY
	My mom does this for dad and
	he just loves it. Now that's
	something you two have in

	common.

ROM
I'm afraid that's all, my sweet
love. Remember that your dad
said that we can't get married
till, till, ah—-!
JENNY
Till you fly. Yeah, he's only
being funny. I know he'll do
whatever mom wants and she likes
you a lot.
Rom holds Jenny's hands as he rises with a turn to face her.
ROM
I bet she wouldn't like me if
she saw my hair this messed.
She laughs. Rom holds Jenny's hands in front of his chest by his heart.
JENNY
Well! You have nice thick

clean hair. And you're the
first boy I ever met,

besides my little brother,
who doesn't have dandruff.
Rom smiles warmly.
ROM
That's the nicest thing I've

   Every heard.

JENNY
Well its true.
ROM
Why does your father speak of

   Marriage the first time I walk
   into the house? He's funny.

JENNY
That's because everybody I've ever
met proposed on the second date.
ROM
How many is that?
JENNY
Oh about ten. Your number
(pause) eleven.
Rom kisses Jenny.
They stare into their eyes a while.
FADE TO:

EXT. INDIAN TOWN - DAY
(Dream Scene)
In her eyes she sees herself, the little girl in white riding on top of a small elephant. Little Rom sits behind.
They wave at the people standing along side the road as he passes. They wave back along a big parade.
FADE TO:
EXT. CITY TOWN - DAY
(DREAM SCENE)
Rom sees in his minds eye pretty little Jenny riding a top of an elephant float in a parade, waving to the people at
the side of the road. He's in front and she is behind him.
People wave back and cheer waving small flags.
FADE TO:

EXT. ROOF TOP - DAY

Rom and Jenny release their hug and sit down on the rug to eat lunch.

After each takes a big bite out of the others sub sandwich, he smiles at her and she at him.

He extends his sub for her to bite and then she to him.

Rom and Jenny stuff their puffed out cheeks, then laugh.

EXT. HART TOWNHOUSE - DAY

Tommy rushes out the front door, down the steps and away down the street heading back to school for his last two classes.

He carries one book in his hand and a small pad of paper.

Across the street behind a van we see the three hoods watching the front door.

HOOD #1

She ain't ever coming out!

HOOD #1

She might be doing her hair

and that might take forever.

HOOD #3

Yeah forever!

Hood No.2 slaps Hood No. 3 on the head.

HOOD #1

Then why don't we just kidnap

her brother? Yeah sure! That's

just as ee-fective. Right boys?

Hood No. 2 and Hood No. 3 shake their heads up and down repeatedly like bobble head toys.

Hood No.1 swiftly punches both guys in their stomachs.

The two Hoods bend over in pain.

HOOD #1

OK. Lets go. He's getting too

far ahead of us now.

(CHASE-FOLLOWING TYPE SCENARIOS)

The three move off after Tommy.

Hoods Nos. 2 &3 rub their stomachs as they scamper along the parked cars.

Suddenly, at the middle of the block, Tommy turns and crosses through the back yards.

He jumps several fences, wooden slat, picked, stockade and lastly chain link.

The first Hood clears the fences with no problem.

The second and third hood fall over each fence ripping their jacket sleeves, pant pockets, hitting their heads together.

Wooden slat—Rip, Rip, Knock, Knock!

Picked fence—Rip, Rip, Knock, Knock!

Stockade fence—Rip, Rip, Knock, Knock! Thud, thud!

Chain link fence—Rip, Rip, Knock, Knock! Thud!

HOOD #3

Hey I'm caught. Help! Get me

off, I'm hanging here. Help!

Guys, help!

Hood No.1 and Hood No.3 go back to unhook No.3 off the fence.

Tommy now trots down the next block and soon is near town.

He short cuts through a mini mall by entering the big drug store.

Hood No.1 crosses through the traffic. Hoods No.2 and No.3 get side swiped by a bus pulling out from the curb.

Water splashes them in the face. They wipe it off.

All three hoods enter the mall.

Each trips over the other as they go through the doors.

INT. MALL - DAY

Tommy rushes through the store past the afternoon crowd.

Out into the hallway and on towards the other entrance way

down on the other end.

As the hoods follow, Hood No. 1 knocks over a few cartons of gumballs. They break open and spill all over.

Hoods Nos. 2 & 3 slip and fall down several times.

TWO DOZEN PATRONS look over at them and shake their heads.

Down the hallway the hoods rush, stumbling here and there into people.

The hoods bump into the hot dog cart, jewelry cart and

scarf cart causing a commotion.

We See Tommy exit the mall heading down the street to the high school.

The Hoods collide together at the exit door and fall down on to the mall rubber mat.

SIX PEOPLE enter mall, they kick and step on Hoods #2 & #3.

Both boys moan and groan over and over in pain.

They finally get up and stumble through the door to the outside curb.

Hood #1 points at Tommy moving away in the distance.

EXT. STREET - DAY

Tommy hops on the back ledge of a bread truck pulling away.

The Hoods watch Tommy and smack their heads as he continues to keep way ahead of them.

Tommy hops off the truck as it stops at the corner light by the High School, two blocks down.

Tommy jogs up the steps and into the school hallway.

The hoods arrive at the steps a few seconds later, out of breath, looking like the cat dragged them in from the garbage dump.

The three sit on the curb to rest. Hood # 3 falls asleep on Hood #2. Hood #3 mumbles in his sleep.

HOOD #3

Was I picking my nose Mom?

Hood #1 squeezes Hood#3 on the nose. He wakes up.

INT. SCHOOL HALLWAY - DAY

Tommy goes down hall and cuts through the cafeteria.

SEVERAL KIDS nod at Tommy as he passes by.

We see the Hoods enter and spot Tommy as he enters the Cafeteria. A minute later they are in the cafeteria. They stand a little up from the door as the bell rings.

HOOD #1

It's the last class for the day.

HOOD #2

Yeah. Last one. Where is he?

The bell goes off and the students rise and rush out madly.

HOOD #3

Yeah. Ohhhhh, brother!

The Hoods get knocked over, food such as soup-salad-ketchup covered fries get dumped over them while the students trample over the three who are lying on their backs.

TWO FEMALE STUDENTS toss their trays on top of them.

STUDENT #1

Get the heck out of the way

you bums!

She kicks one Hood viciously.

STUDENT #2

Leave her alone you jerks. Who

let you in here anyway? Look out

I'm late.

She smacks Hood #3 over the head with her tray.

He falls down again.

Then she tosses the tray on Hood #2 who continues to slip on the French fries.

Hood No.1 finally gets to his feet. He looks around the empty cafeteria and shakes his head at the other two.

HOOD#3 looks up. He has a ketchup package stuck in each nostril.

HOOD #1

He got away. Damn he's fast!

Well, we'll have to get him

later. He can't get away from

us forever. Come on, let's

get out of here boys. (Fists)

Hood No.2 and Hood No.3 are on their knees when Hood No. 1 whacks them each hard in the head.

They both slip down again onto the floor.

INT. SHOP CLASS - DAY

Tommy rushes in through the door and down to his desk.

The SHOP TEACHER enters from the end door and smiles at the class. The SHOP STUDENTS hoot as he enters. He smiles.

SHOP TEACHER

I'm glad to say your projects

have all been marked and your
all passing.

The class cheers.
Tommy takes out a stick of gum. He unwraps it.
SHOP TEACHER
Our next project is a TV Guide

rack. Something you all can use,
I'm sure. -—Or you can sell it.

Tommy sticks the gum in his mouth and stares out the window.
He sees the three Hoods rushing over the grass toward the corner.
They stumble into the statue of President Grant and fall down over each other. He points and laughs.
The SHOP TEACHER sees the three Hoods fall down too.

SHOP TEACHER
Maybe we should make something for
those three guys out there, Tommy.
TOMMY
Yeah. Like what?
STUDENT
Like three seeing-eye canes.

Just to help them get around
the school grounds. Ha! Ha!

Everyone laughs at the three Hoods outside.
They collide and stumble along their way.

INT. SEVEN ELEVEN STORE - DAY
We see the Suited Man return to the store and look
around for Rom. Finally he walks over to Wayne who's standing behind the counter.
SUITED MAN
So where is your boss today?
WAYNE
He's out for lunch. I think
he'll be back after two.
SUITED MAN
Are you sure? I was here this
morning.
WAYNE
Yep! Want a paper or lotto ticket?

Suited man smiles and removes a letter from his top pocket.
He hands it to the boy.
SUITED MAN
No, I don't think I'll need

   anything like that anymore.
   Here. Give this to your boss.
   This will make his day.

The boy puts the envelope on the counter and shakes his head sarcastically as the man exits out of the Seven Eleven store.
Once gone, the boy lifts the letter up to the light and tries to see through it, but can't see anything.
He puts it with a stack of mail off to the side of the cash register.
Then, just as the teen lifts up a hot dog, the phone rings.
The boy jumps and jabs his eye with the end of the wiener.
Half blinded, the teen reaches over to lift the Phone.
WAYNE
Hello! No! This is not Harry's
Strudel Shop. And the same to
you guy.
The teen slams the phone down on his hot dog and the ketchup splashes all over his face. His foot slips on something behind the counter and he falls back down and out of sight, grabbing for the phone cord.
The phone falls down on his head, lastly.
WAYNE
Woow! Opps! Owe! (ring-thud!)
oh—-!
We see his two feet rise up above the counter, then drop down out of sight. (Real loud thud)

EXT. SCHOOL YARD - DAY
The three Hoods stand by a side alley just a short ways down from the school. They are wiping themselves clean with a towel.
They hear the last class bell ring and huddle together like a football team does bent over, hands on knees.
HOOD #1
We don't have to catch him or
beat him up boys. Think.
HOOD #2
Why not?
HOOD #3
Yeah? Why not?
Hood No. 1 smacks the other two lightly.
They huddle closer.
(We see the dumb faces from inside huddle)
HOOD #1

Now listen up, dog brains. We
just tell him his sister needs
to bring some kind of papers
home and that she's at my house
helping out my sister.
HOOD #2
Gee! I never met your sister.
Is she pretty?
Hood No.1 smacks Hood No.3 who smacks No.2 in the head.
HOOD #1
I don't have a sister cucumber
brain! Now, we lead him to my
Uncles basement and tie him up
once we get him there. It is
a brilliant plan-o. -—Right?
The other two shake their heads yes, then no.
Then they bump heads as they stand straight.
HOOD #1
Hey! Here he comes now, behind
those girls.
Three girls pass by on the sidewalk and then Tommy follows.
Soon the three are up and behind Tommy.
HOOD #1
Hey buddy! Is your sister
called Jenny?
Tommy stops and turns with a clenched fist.
TOMMY
Yeah! What of it?
Hood No. 1 puts his hands in the air.
The other two Hoods step back.
HOOD #1
Well she's with my sister and
told us to tell, I mean ask you
to bring some papers or something
home for her. That's all. OK?
Tommy lowers his fist.
TOMMY
Well, where do you live?
HOOD #1
Not too far. Just follow us
and we'll take good care of
you buddy boy. I ah, always
do what my dear sister asks.
Don't you?

TOMMY
Yeah! Sometimes I do. I
guess it's that lesson plan
thing she's been typing up
all week. OK, go ahead and
I'll follow.
The three hoods walk off, winking to each other. Hood No.3 covers his mouth to hide his smirk. Tommy follows behind them. Down the street into an alley they head.
HOOD #1
Short cut. We'll go in through
the basement when we get there!
TOMMY
Ah huh!
They all disappear out of view into the basement.

EXT. APARTMENT STEPS - DAY
Rom and Jenny walk down the steps hand in hand. The LANDLORD, Mister Pitt who is holding a bag of groceries passes by and stops to talk.

Mister Pitt

I heard the phone ringing in the
hallway and answered it early
this morning.
ROM
Was it for me?
Mister Pitt
Yes, it was your brother. He said
that your dad is sending you two
pair of Italian shoes.
ROM
Oh yes. Oh, let me introduce my
girlfriend Jenny Hart. Jenny,
this is my landlord. He is one
of my closest friends.
Jenny and the Landlord shake hands. The old Landlord pats Rom on the back and shoulder as he walks up the steps.
Mister Pitt
Rom is the nicest guy on the
block. He's what my wife calls
a keeper. Rom, if the package
arrives when you're at work, I'll
sign for it.
Rom waves and smiles up to his friend. [FOLLOWING]
ROM
Thanks. That will be great.
Rom and Jenny walk down the sidewalk, hand in hand.
JENNY
He's a nice old man isn't he?
ROM
Yes! He was returning from India
on my plane one year ago. He let
me stay here for nothing until
I got my job at the 7-11 store.
JENNY
Guys like him are rare. That's...
ROM
He's a boy-scout leader too.
JENNY
Nice man.
They head down the alley and stop halfway to hug and kiss.
Jenny then heads for home.
Rom heads towards the 7-11 store.

INT. BASEMENT - DAY

We See the three hoods enter the basement followed by Tommy.

Just as Hood #1 pulls a ceiling light string, Hood #2 tosses a rope around Tommy and Hood #3 wraps the rope around the two about a basement pole.

Hood #1 smacks Hood #3 and grabs the rope. He grabs another rope and places it around Tommy's struggling head and pulls it up through the ceiling beam, tying it onto two large nails.

Tommy kicks Hood #3 in the groin.

Hood #2 swings at Tommy but smacks Hood #3 on the knee.

This causes a jerk reaction and he now gets kicked in the groin.

Hood #2 and Hood #3 hop about holding their crotches.

Hood #1 then winds a thick rope about Tommy several times, and around the pole, pinning Tommy's arms to his side.

TOMMY

What are you guys, nuts?

HOOD #1

No! We just have to teach
Rom and Jenny who's territory
this is and to pay up. If they
don't you just stay here and
starve. Now we will be back
for you later, buddy boy.

HOOD #2

Yeah, later, mop head.

HOOD #3

Yeah. Starve your ass, baby
Face. Be back later.

The three hoods head out the back basement door into the backyard.

The Hoods leave their sunglasses on the bench next to Tommy.

Tommy begins to struggle. He twists and the beam breaks. The neck rope pulls free of the nails too and falls off.

Next he sees a plug connected to the grinder.

He grabs the sunglasses and tosses them inside the grinder.

He untangles the rope about his neck.

Tommy spots a new looking lawnmower sitting off to the side and then wheels it out the back door, laughing with delight.

Tommy then returns.

Tommy grabs a coffee can of grease and empties it onto the bottom step.

He gives it a kiss – wave goodbye.

Then Tommy tosses the coffee can up at the light, breaking it. He then leaves the basement.

INT. SEVEN ELEVEN STORE - DAY

Rom enters the store and then pays Wayne for the week. He gives him an extra five bucks and the teen gives him a friendly, short pound on the shoulder with his fist.

ROM

You deserve a tip. Keep up

the good work, Wayne.

WAYNE

Thanks a lot boss. Oh there's

a letter some guy left.

Wayne exits the shop but pokes his head back inside for one additional remark.

WAYNE

Oh! He said thank you?

Rom shakes his head.

The boy disappears.

Rom walks over to the counter and grabs the mail. He reads several envelopes. He then places all but one away in a slot.

As he begins to open the envelope, the three Hoods enter the store.

They stand by the entrance together, side-by- side.

Each pounds his fists and acts tough in front of the other.

Rom is startled momentarily.

He thought they were never coming back.

HOOD #1

You're gonna pay up. We have

your girlfriend's brother. If
you know what's good for you,
you'll pay up right now. And
we mean now, buster.

HOOD #2

And that includes last week too.

HOOD #3

(unlit cigar in mouth)

And three hot-dogs too! With

mustard and onions. (thud-thud)
Owe! Owe!

Hood #1 smacks Hood #2, then Hood #2 smacks Hood #3.

Rom lowers his head He then stops. Behind the hood he sees Tommy through the window, merrily pushing a lawnmower down the sidewalk.

His eyebrows rise up as his lips form a whistle shape.

Rom calmly goes to the register and removes some cash.

He heads around the counter, standing at arms length.

All three Hoods extend their hands and snicker.

A moment passes. Rom holds out the cash with one hand and the other remains behind his back.

They reach out and he steps back.

They reach out again and he steps back a little more.

Suddenly, he sprays the three in the eyes with whip cream.

Just as before, the three rush out into the street, half blind. They bang into each other as they rush away.

Rom boots Hood #3 in the ass, as he exits last. He then sprays his ass additionally.

Rom holds door and yells out loudly.

ROM

If you want some more come
back again! I'm holding
your hot-dogs hostage! You
cucumbers! Go back to school!

Rom closes the glass door and laughs as the three stumble into the back of a dump truck momentarily stopped at the corner. The driver pulls away and they fall down again.

INT. HART TOWNHOUSE - DAY

We see Jenny enter the kitchen and sit down next to her mom. Mother Hart slides half of her sandwich in front of Jenny.

Jenny rises and grabs a clean glass off the dishwasher rack.

Jenny sits, grabs the pitcher of tea and then fills her glass.

MOTHER HART

So how is your new boyfriend?

JENNY

Rom is the nicest man I've
ever met! He cares for me
and is a gentleman.

MOTHER HART

I can see you two together. It
was like that with your father.
After we met, he was over at
my house every spare moment.
I think he didn't want the other
fly boys to talk to me. Kind
of monopolizing my time cause
he was crazy over me.

She nips on the sandwich and waits for Jenny's reply.

Jenny chews and takes a drink. She swallows in a hurry.

JENNY

Rom wants to go steady but he's
not very rich and it bothers him.
If he gets over that male thing,
we can get more serious. Right
now I have strong feelings.

MOTHER HART
You slept restless last night.
Was it the job opportunity?
JENNY
It was last week but, no, I
dreamt of India and Palaces
and beautiful carpets and then
I met up with several mean,
tigers who tried to eat me
and that's when I woke up.

MOTHER HART
That sounds bad.

JENNY

I've never had a bad dream
like that before. I'm afraid
that something bad is going to
happen to me or to Rom.
Jenny takes another big bite out of her sandwich.
MOTHER HART
I used to eat like that when
I was engaged, just like that.
You usually eat very slow, girl.
I'd say we may have a bit of
Indian in the family soon.
Mother Beck pokes Jenny softly in the side for fun.
Jenny squirms just as Tommy comes in the back door.
MOTHER HART
So why do you look so happy?
Tommy stands by the hallway door to the basement and covers the smile on his face with one hand.
TOMMY
Sure am. I got, won a new free
lawnmower. It was complimentary.
JENNY
Oh that's not nice.
TOMMY
Nice bit of luck. A kind of dumb
meatball luck. Yeah, meatballs!
Jenny looks at her brother seriously. Mom doesn't catch on to anything.
JENNY

You stay clear away from those

Hoods. They are dangerous.

Tommy laughs at Jenny's remark and heads down the steps.

Mother Hart looks at Jenny and shrugs her shoulders.

MOTHER HART

You better tell Rom about these
guys the next time you see him.
By the way, he was here at lunch
time and fixed the mower for your
Dad. That will please him.

Jenny walks to the basement door and yells down.

JENNY

(yelling).

Don't fool with those meatballs.

Jenny looks at her mom and sighs.

JENNY

I'll tell him tonight at the
Zoo. Two baby elephants were
born and they will be providing
extra lighting to see them.

MOTHER HART

We can meet you there. Dad will
want to meet Rom again and thank
him for fixing the lawn-mower.
Maybe he'll smile. He never smiles
anymore, not since the accident.

JENNY

I'm gonna shower and do my
hair for tonight.

Mother Beck gives out a slight grin.

MOTHER HART

Well, it's been quite some time
since you did your hair before
a date. My, my, my! (points)

Jenny giggles and rushes down the hall and (THUMP-THUMP-THUMP) up the stairs.

EXT. HOODS TOWNHOUSE - DAY

The Hoods return to the back basement door, which was left open.

HOOD #2

That man is getting me angry
as a pig in cement. I swear!

HOOD #3

I can't see yet. Let me go
down stairs first.

HOOD #1

Go! Go! Get down there.

Hood No.3 goes down the steps first. Hood No.3 hits the light switch just as he steps on the auto grease left on the bottom step by Tommy.

HOOD #3

Wow-We! (crunch, smash)

Hood No.2 follows next. He flicks the light switch several times. No light goes on, since Tommy smashed it out.

Hood No.2 steps down, holding his bleary eyes with his other hand.

HOOD #2

Yoah! Yoooooaaah! (smash-bing!)

Hood No.1 now rushes ahead and he too slips away into the dark of the basement.

HOOD #1

Hey! Hey—-! (thud, thud, bong)

HOOD #2

Owe!

HOOD #3

Yeah! Owe, owe! I want mommy.

Silence. We see (and hear) steam roll out of the basement doorway.

HOOD #1

(loudly spoken)

Is that your foot or mine?

Is that my arm or yours?

Silence.

HOOD #1

Don't bite my arm, or my leg!

(CRUNCH-CRUNCH)

HOOD #2

Owe, my foot!

HOOD #3

Owe, my arm!

HOOD #1

Sorry boys. Oh – my - head!

A stray dog arrives and walks to the basement step, then lifts it's leg near the doorway.

HOOD #2

Hey stop spitting on me and get up.

I smell monkey.

HOOD #3

I'm not spitting. You spit right

in my eye. Pee-uh! You smell!

The dog smiles and moves away.

FADE TO:

EXT. TOWNHOUSE – EARLY EVENING

We See Tommy head out the door, down the steps and then down the street.

The three, bandaged Hoods are near-by and watch from behind an old cargo van.

Tommy goes to the side of the building and then carries two trashcans to the street.

He pounds one of the lids on with his fists.

From behind, the Hoods toss a bag over his head and drag Tommy into the van. (Bag and rope around body)

The Hoods scamper into the van after they slap hands.

They hurt each other's bandaged hands doing it. (Stoop over in pain)

The van soon drives off, swerving all over the street.

INT. BEAUTY SALOON - DAY

In the beauty salon chair, the teenage Girl, Katie, looks in the mirror and smiles. (Jazzy up-tempo music)

Katie's hair and face has been wonderfully transformed.

The whole STAFF OF TEN HAIR DRESSERS claps as she rises to leave.

The hairdresser blows a bubble and shoves her gum back in her mouth with her thumb, staring hard at Katie's hair.

KATIE

Oh come on. You're making me

  blush, I wish I looked this
  good everyday. Thank you all,
  you're a great bunch of girls.

She leaves a tip.

HAIRDRESSER

(use a cameo - female star here)

Remember, only a touch perfume.

Keep it clean and neat, sweetie.

Swings her purse over her shoulder and dances out the door.

Inside, the women patrons clap as she leaves.

Katie blows a kiss through the front window.

She pulls away in her car. Black fumes spew out.

INT. HOODS TOWNHOUSE - DAY

The Hoods tie Tommy to a living room wing back chair, then pull off his head bag. Hood #2 wraps the rope around him twenty times and ties a knot.

HOOD #1

So you thought you would get

away! You're staying here till
Rom pays up. How's that?

HOOD #2

Yeah! Pays up, Hart. (dumb manner)

HOOD #3

Pays up! Pays up! (dumb manner)

Tommy just smirks. Hood #3 makes a thumbs-up sign and hits his right eye with his thumb.

HOOD #1 circles the chair.

HOOD #1

So, where is the lawnmower?

TOMMY

I left the back door open,
maybe somebody stole it!

HOOD #3

Yeah stole it! Stole it!

Hood No.1 swats Hood No.3.

TOMMY

Hey! How about a juicy burger?
I'll sit here and be good.

Hood #1 pauses and looks at Hoods No.2 and No.3 who look up
with starved expressions. Then they lick their lips.

HOOD #1

Ah. OK. Let's go but we'll
be back quickly so don't try
anything stupid. Ha! Ha!

All three exit out the front door. All goes quiet.
They then return.
Hood No.1 grabs the remote by the TV, snickers.
Hood @1
No entertainment for you.
He shoves it under the couch seat cushion, then leaves.
Tommy just shakes his head.
He slips the chair cushion out from under him, inhales and easily squirms down through the ropes.
Once free, Tommy grabs the remote from under the coach cushion. He then lifts up large plasma Television Set.
TOMMY
(whispers to himself)
What a good gift for my new
girl friend. Katie will just
love me of this. Terrific.
Tommy exits the living room with a grin.
He returns with TV under arm, lifts up the TV cart and exits again.
Through the doorway we see Tommy place the TV set face down on the cart and wheel it away down the sidewalk.
He whistles as he walks onward with a happy, proud gate.

INT. TOWNHOUSE - NIGHT
Jenny walks down the steps to the living room. She sits on the couch and picks up a magazine to read.
Mr. Hart enters. He wheels backward at the sight of his well-dressed daughter.
DADDY HART
You must have a big date tonight!
Not that Rom guy?
JENNEY
Daddy I love him. He fixed your

Lawn mower, you know.

Mr. Hart reads the paper, not showing any emotion.
DADDY BECK
Hmm! I guess he did. Might

be a pretty handy guy to have
around here. We'll see, Jenny.
He seems like a dreamer.

Mr. Hart smiles briefly, then frowns.
He lifts up the paper again to read. He lowers it again.
JENNY
Yes he is! I hope someday we

get engaged. He is so wonderful.

Someday he'll have a rug store.

DADDY HART
(loud with expression))
Is he now? That's pretty good!

  Well, you can marry him when -
  rugs - fly! (pause) Fat chance
  of that my dear daughter.

Jenny rises, grabs her coat, kisses Dad on the cheek, and moves to the front door.
JENNY
You don't really know him yet.
I know in my heart that he is
very special. I know you'll feel
the same way someday too.
Dad peers over the paper briefly.
Looks back down into his paper.
Jenny opens the door.
DADDY HART
Well we will see little angel.

  Be careful out there. You look
  too good tonight. Where's Tommy?

JENNY
Oh no Daddy! I'm just fine.
It's just a few blocks. Later—-
Jenny grabs a letter off the entrance stool, sees it is for her, tucks it in her pocketbook.
She slams the door hard as she leaves.
Mother Hart enters the living room now.
She peeks out the front window.
MOTHER HART
She's gone and I heard how well
you handled her. My goodness!
DADDY HART
Oh all right! Invite the boy

  to supper. I hope he has good
  manners.

Mother tosses a pillow at Dad.
MOTHER HART
Manners my foot. He should see
the way you eat pizza. By the

way, since they are all out,
   lets go out for Pizza and then
   meet Jenny and Rom at the Zoo.

You can look over the new baby
elephant. Oh stop frowning.
DADDY HART
Fine then. Well, lets go.

   I'm starved. I'll promise,
   I'll smile for you tonight.

Daddy Hart rubs his tummy.
Mother Hart pats it and smirks. (The front door opens automatically.)
She hugs him and pushes Dad's wheelchair out the front door.

INT. HOODS TOWNHOUSE - NIGHT
   The Hoods arrive back home and the living room with fast food in hand.
   They find UNCLE MOTSEY sitting on the couch picking his teeth and smiling.
   His partner in crime, scar faced SHIVER, who enters from the kitchen with two bottles of beer in hand. He hands
a bottle to Motsy.
   Beer spills over Shiver's arm and face as he guzzles it down.
HOOD #1
Hey! Where's the kid gone,

   Uncle Motsey?

Uncle Motsey carefully sips his beer.
UNCLE MOTSEY
Kid? I saw no kid in here when
we arrived and the door was wide
open. That's the way you've been
taking care of my house while I
was in the slammer for six months?
(Places bottle on coffee table)
I did see Cheese Whiz and Windex

   on my good bathroom towel. Now it
   stinks bad. Answer that, boys.

SHIVER
Say. Where's the High Deaf Plasma

   TV I stole for your Uncle? You

didn't break, did you?

Hood No.1 looks for the remote in the couch. It's gone.
He looks puzzled. He tosses the bag of burgers on the table.
Hood No.2 and Hood No.3 arrive eating a shared bag of large fries. They stop chewing when Shiver pulls his gun out.

HOOD #1
No they're OK. They are with me,
physically, but not mentally.
UNCLE MOTSEY
What's the explanation here?
Hood No.1 sits down in front of Uncle Motsey on a stool. He's tongue tied.
Shiver lowers his gun and the other Hoods relax in place.
Hood #3 extends the fries to Shiver.
He just turns his face away and sneers back at the boy.
The fries fall to the floor. Hood No.3 picks several up and stuffs them in his mouth.
Hood No.1 frowns at Hood No.3 .
Shiver finger flicks the both of them on their heads.
They sit still. Hood #1 explains all to his Uncle, sitting next to him on the sofa.
HOOD #1
The boys and me tried to get a
donation from the Seven Eleven
guy but he refuses. So we grab
his girl friends brother but he
escapes from the basement. The
boys and I re-grab him and then

  return here and he's gone. So is
  the new lawnmower and the TV stuff.

SHIVER
So you saw him take them?
HOOD #1
Well no Mister Shiver. The
basement door was open like
the front door. Shit, we
tied him up real well too.
UNCLE MOTSEY
Oh. He might have had a friend.
Did the bar and the Pizza shop
pay up?
Hood No.2 sneezes on Shiver.
Shiver wipes himself.
His face gets red.

SHIVER
Hey! Now that wasn't nice.

    Now I'm splattered with chewed
    up fries and snot. You could
    have turned away, kid. I think
    the kid that took the stuff
    should work for us. Let's dump
    these monkeys.

HOOD #2
Monkeys are mean. -—Sorry man!
Shiver puts down his beer, turns toward Hood No.2 and grabs his sides, turning him upside down. He bangs his head on the floor a few times.
HOOD #2
Whooah! Help! Help!
HOOD #1
Hey! Put him down!
UNCLE MOTSEY
(smiling now)
Oh let him have some fun. He's
just teaching your friend some
good manners.
Uncle Motsey calmly watches Shiver's actions.
SHIVER
(bear hug)
I'm sure it was an accident. I
think what you need is your nose
cleaned out a bit. Don't worry,
I'll do it for you for free kid.
Hood #2 spits out all his food on the floor. Shiver tosses him against the wall but holds on to him still.
Shiver then strolls down the hall towards the bathroom.
Hood No.3 gulps his fries down as he gets out of the way.
HOOD #2 (OS)
I won't do it again. I promise.
We hear a toilet bowl flush and some gargling noises.
Uncle Motsey puts up his hand when Hood No. 1 rises. He sits back down.
Shortly afterward, Shiver returns holding Hood No.2. He's still upside down. His head and hair are soaking wet and dripping.
Shiver turns him back upright and sets him down on his feet.
Uncle Motsey and the others laugh heartily at the sight.
Hood No.2 runs back into the bathroom to throw up.
The toilet flushes loudly. (We hear him heaving)
Uncle Motsey chuckles louder, slapping his sides.

Uncle Motsey picks up the TV guide and tosses it at Hood #2 as he reenters the living room. He has a towel wrapped around his head.

Hood No. 2 falls back over a sofa stool onto his ass.

UNCLE MOTSEY

Now what you did was good kid.

But what you should have done
is this. One, make sure the
girl's Dad ain't a cop. Then
two, grab her or better yet

make a good example of her.

Windex and cheese whiz won't
protect the Seven Eleven man

from us. He's history, boys!

SHIVER

You three look a little soft
and squeamish to me. Does

the sight of blood make any

of you sick?

UNCLE MOTSEY

Boys. Rom and his girl will

soon disappear. (pause) Shiver,
never send boys to do a man's
job. We nab her and bamb-oh.

(fist) Ha! Ha! Ha! Ha! ...

All three Hoods shake their heads left and right, mouths opened wide. Uncle Motsey pulls out a huge Bowie Knife.

Uncle Motsey (laughing evilly) tosses the knife across the room into a picture on the wall of Grandma Mosses.

It sticks in by her ass. (We hear sinister organ music)

Shiver and Uncle Motsey laugh over and over, holding up their beers proudly, toasting the plan.

The Hoods just nervously stand there and shake in their boots, heads shaking up and down like bobble head toys.

EXT. YELLOW PORCH - NIGHT

We see Tommy knock on Katie's front door. Katie comes outside her ranch house. The front porch is quite wide.

She closes the door, kisses Tommy. She then leads him over to the swinging glider, a two-seat deck chair.

Tommy points to the TV set handing on the edge of the porch He plugs it into the outside electric socket. A TV cable extension has been hooked up from the side of the house.

The girl puts her hands around Tommy's neck. They kiss.

Tommy turns on the set. Both watch as they swing back and forth on the glider. No one utters a word.

From behind, Katie's PARENTS draw back the living room curtains, sitting on the couch. They also watch the two kids who are watching the Television set. Mom and Dad slap hands.

The father lights his pipe and smiles over to the mom whose busy knitting a yellow/blue scarf, peeking up off and on at the Plasma TV screen.

INT. SEVEN ELEVEN STORE - NIGHT

We See the street sign on the corner of the store property which reads 'Seventh and Eleventh' streets.

Back inside the store, Wayne arrives through the front door. He soon sits on a stool behind the cash register counter.

Rom heads out and back into his office, then out, holding two boxes of round shaped light bulbs.

WAYNE

Should I close up later if you

don't get back boss?

ROM

I'm sure I'll be back later.

I need to put brighter bulbs

up on the roof of my apartment,

for safety. Maybe I'll throw

a party up there someday.

WAYNE

Sounds like an idea. I hope

it starts after eleven so I can

come too.

ROM

Oh I will close at seven that

night but you will get paid

through eleven.

WAYNE

Yeah that's great. Do it

real soon, boss.

Rom gives the boy a parting wave as he exits the store heading down the left alley towards his apartment house.

The teenage boy flips a wooden hand brush up into the air in the store. It comes down and hits him in the head. (Bonk!)

He falls off his stool down behind the counter.

We see Wayne's feet rise up over the counter and rest on the counter top, We See the left boot is on the right foot and the right boot is on the left. (Angle On)

WAYNE (OS)

Why do my feet ache so much

 today?

His feet wiggle.

EXT. ALLEY - NIGHT
Rom moves out of sight through the rear apartment entrance.
Uncle Motsey, Shiver and the three HOODS arrive. They stand hidden out of sight behind the garbage canister. The hoods stand behind the older men.
Motsey picks up an old wooden chair in the alley. He smashes it apart and grabs a sidepiece as a weapon.
Shiver violently blasts his fist through another chairs wooden seat, splitting it in half. He smacks his side arm.
Motsey grins evilly at the boys who act startled.
Hood No.3 bumps No.2 into No.1 into Shiver. Shiver socks No.1 and all three young hoods fall over. The big trash bin door swings open, vegetable garbage spills out and down onto the boys. They rolls around and get up with food stains all over them. Hood #3 holds his nose.
Uncle Motsey and Shiver move into the dark shadows to wait.
Shiver grabs Hood$2 and #3 by the ears and pulls them out of the streetlight and into the shadow.
Hood #3 watches, then he quickly jumps into the shadow.

EXT. APARTMENT ROOF - NIGHT
We see Rom enter the roof and place a package down on his rug. As he begins to change out the light bulbs just as the landlord, Mister Pitt arrives.
PITT
Oh! I thought I saw you come
up here. New light bulbs!
Good.
ROM
Yes new bulbs to make it safe.

 They are energy savers too.

Rom screws in the last bulb, then reaches into the brown bag and pulls out a long string of Christmas lights, which the landlord helps to raise up and around the corner light poles.
PITT
Say Rom, are you throwing a

 party up here?

Rom smiles as he ties the last string on near the entrance door by the electric, out-door socket. Pitt plugs them into the socket by the door.
ROM
Well maybe a small one if, if....

PITT
If you get engaged?
ROM
Yes! Good luck my friend.
PITT
Well, turn off the lights
when you leave but keep the
Christmas lights on for me.
ROM
I will turn off the lights

   for sure. On at eleven and
   off at seven.

The landlord pats Rom on the back. He then hits the light switch and the roof lights up in a colorful rainbow of glowing and twinkling lights under the stars.
They smile as they glance around.
PITT
Only you would think of something
like this. Oh, your package from

   home is in my kitchen. I'll go
   get it. See you a little later.

The Landlord exits the roof. Rom heads over to his big rug.
He sits and reads the bulb box information.

EXT. APARTMENT ALLEY - NIGHT
We see Jenny walk into the alley, heading towards the Seven Eleven Store.
Out from behind the trash bin, all five men leap forward.
Jenny is startled and freezes in place.
She moves back till she is flat up against the dark green metal trash bin. Motsey drops his wooden weapon.
UNCLE MOTSEY
So you're the little lady that

   this Indian Romish guy is seeing.
   Just your bad luck sister. Grab
   her boys. She's a small one.

Uncle Motsey pulls his knife.
Shiver grabs Jenny's arm by the elbow and pulls it back tightly, gritting his teeth mean like.
Motsey pulls out a rope and knife. He cuts it in half with a switchblade and puts the knife away.
Jenny yells and screams for help but Uncle Motsey covers her mouth.
He then rips her pretty dress up the middle of her chest. She struggles, eyes open wide in fear.

She kicks him and hits but he just smiles down at her.
Jenny's chest is half exposed. Shiver pushes her down.
The Hoods and Shiver laugh over her, standing in a huddle.

EXT. APARTMENT ROOF - NIGHT
Rom hears the screams, so he rises and crawls out over the roof ledge to look down.

He frowns at what he sees, then gets real mad and stands up.

He sees Jenny and the Hoods below but then gets dizzy and spins around almost falling off the roof. The Landlord
arrives behind him and grabs him just in time.

Rom lands square on his back in the middle of the rug.

The Landlord drops a package meant for Rom onto the roof.

The Landlord looks over the wall. He looks three times,
a triple take, in disbelief when he sees the gang attacking helpless Jenny.
PITT
Hey! Hey down there. You

    stop that. Stop that right
    now. You bums!

The Landlord turns and leans down over Rom's quivering body.
He lifts him off the rug and shakes him repeatedly.
Rom just mutters aloud. He seems to be in shock.
ROM
The elephant threw me off Grandpa.
He's going to step on me, he's
going to step on me. I'm scared!
PITT
Snap out of it! There's no elephant!
You're on the roof! Your girl

    friend needs you. She's in big
    trouble. Snap out of it Rom.

Your on the roof. Help Jenny.

    You must help Jenny. Rom?
    Romish? Wake up man. (slap)

Rom finally snaps out of it and grabs the Landlord's arms.
ROM
It was the fall. I was scared
from the fall I'm OK now! I'm...
The Landlord releases Rom and then rushes off the roof.
PITT

I'll go call the cops. Don't

worry. There's a car down
the street.

Rom moves back to the ledge and looks down again.

EXT. APARTMENT ALLEY - NIGHT
We see Hood No.1 grab Jenny's shoes from off her feet. She covers her face for protection.
Hood No.2 and Hood #3 stand behind Uncle Motsey.
HOOD #1
Too bad your boyfriend didn't
pay up girl. Guess what's
going to happen to you. Get

her in the van. Tie her up.

Uncle Motsey grabs one of the shoes while the other is tossed up into the air. It falls down on HOOD #1 who falls on #2 and #3.
HOOD #2
(On his back)
Hey boss! Some guy on the roof
is yelling down at us.
UNCLE MOTSEY
Who cares! We've got a job to

do and this is just the start.

Uncle Motsey grabs a small piece of Jenny's hair and cuts it off with his knife.
UNCLE MOTSEY
A souvenir. I always keep a

souvenir. Ha! Ha! Ha! Hey
Shiver. Your turn!

Shiver lifts her up. He then tosses Jenny on his shoulders. She pounds his chest to no avail. He spins her around.
Shiver laughs as he slaps her bottom several times.
Jenny screams and somehow slips down free again.
Shiver loosens his belt. He starts to unbutton his shirt next.
SHIVER

Don't play with me, little bitch!

Uncle Motsey laughs. The other Hoods gather closer around Shiver and Jenny.
Hood No.1 tries to cover Jenny's mouth and she bites him.

Shiver laughs and she spits in his face. She rises up.

Motsey pushes Jenny down real hard again.

She sits up dazed and in a momentary stupor.

EXT. APARTMENT ROOF - NIGHT

Rom falls back on the rug on his knees.

He looks up to the stars and cries out with tears in his eyes.

ROM

Please God. Help me save my

girl. Help me save the one

I love. Please father above.

A moment of silence passes and we hear a distant scream.

JENNY (OS)

Rom! Help me! Rom my love,

help me! Someone, help me!

A stream of sparkle looking dust falls about the roof from the heavens above. Suddenly the carpet shakes and rises.

Additional star beams glow and lower onto the roof.

The static electric light beams seem to surround the carpet. It stiffens, then, it rises slowly up two feet in the air.

Rom stands up. He gets his balance, legs spread out wide.

He stretches out his hands like superman. (Eyes closed)

ROM

Up and away! Up and away!

The carpet vibrates but does not move.

Rom shakes his head and arms in disgust.

ROM

What is happening here? It

works for Superman! Oh darn.

Rom looks down. The carpet now rises seven feet off the roof above the Christmas lights.

Rom can see the Seven Eleven Store in the distance below.

Rom snaps his fingers, smiles, folds his arms and then shouts aloud. His eyes see the seven eleven street sign and the seven eleven store sign. (WE HEAR special fast paced Orchestra Music, which intensifies for the flying.)

ROM

(joyously)

I got it! I got it now! Yes I do.

Yes Grandpa. Seven Eleven Away!

The carpet takes off over the roof and down into the alley.

It lowers and with lightning speed, smashes against all the hoods sending each into the trash bin and against the brick wall. They are all knocked near senseless.

Uncle Motsey is sent flying head first into the trash bin. His feet stick up high in a 'V' shape.

The legs wiggle and then stop in the straight up, stiff position.

Rom extends his hand and without hesitation, Jenny wipes the tears out of her eyes and grabs on tight. She leaps onto the carpet and hugs Rom. They kiss briefly. He points upward.

Then, just as Jenny looks down, the carpet moves skyward.

The rug hesitates at about rooftop level and rotates half a turn, pointing toward the Zoo lights in the distance just above the Seven Eleven Store.

Shiver wakes up now and pulls out his hidden gun. He shoots at them five times but the bullets deflect off.

A loud police siren startles him and the guns slips away.

Two police cars enter the alley. (One at each end.)

The cars skid to a halt. The policemen exit out fast.

Shiver watches the cars, grabs the gun and takes dead aim.

Shiver finally fires several rounds again, but the bullets just bounce off away from the rug.

He looks into the barrel of the gun in disbelief.

Rom and Jenny peek down over the edge of the rug.

The Hoods rise up. We see that all three got hit in the ass with a rebounding bullet.

They jump up- one, two, three holding their backsides.

Rom laughs, then points toward the Zoo and the oriental-rug speeds away into the night.

The four POLICEMEN electric shock phase, then handcuff each of the gang.

Each hood falls to the ground, shaking like a fish.

Crash! Crash! Crash! Each hood falls in front of the trash bin, quivering from electric shock on the ground. (We see sizzling electricity bounce about each one.)

An officer grabs the gun away from Shiver while another cuffs him. He stands there, stunned.

Moffey's feet just wiggle in the air.

Shiver stares upward in disbelief, mouth frozen open.

Shiver falls back on his knees in shock.

The police smile while they haul him over to a police car.

Landlord Pitt runs out of the back door and salutes the police.

He's holding a baby pet monkey in his arms.

(Angle on the Monkey holding onto Mister Pitt)

EXT. CITY SKY - NIGHT
   [SPACED OUT HERE TO THE END FOR THE SEVERAL FLYING SCENES]

We see Rom and Jenny kiss as the carpet fly's high into the sky.

Rom folds his arms and they head down towards the bright lights at the Zoo where the crowd is viewing a newborn baby elephant.

Daddy and Mother Hart are there, looking from the front rail.

Suddenly, Rom and Jenny float into sight above the Indian elephants below.

The crowd begins to roar and clap.

Jenny waves down at Mom and dad.

Daddy Hart looks up and his eyes open wide.

Suddenly he rises out of his wheelchair and stands up.
    (Slow motion – Angle On) (Loud violin music here)

Daddy Hart waves at Jenny, then stares down at his legs.

Tears fill his eyes. Tears fall down his cheeks.

Mother Hart shakes uncontrollably and steps back in shock. (Angle On)

She shakes in disbelief all over her body once more.

When She gets her breath back, she then hugs Daddy Heart tightly and gives him a big kiss on the cheek. They hold hands.

The local TV camera (TV CREW OF FIVE) turns off the baby elephant to capture the special event with Daddy Hart.

Then the camera turns upward (ONE MAN POINTS) to the clear dark sky above and zooms in on the hovering rug holding Rom and Jenny.

Tears fill both parents eyes and they cling tight to each other in disbelief of the double miracle.

The four elephants stand up on hind legs. Each animal salutes Rom and Jenny, waving their trunks upward.

A TV ANCHORWOMAN and crew move up behind the Harts.

They film the flying carpet and the Harts.
MOTHER HART
(still drying her tears)
Well how's that for flying, Pop?

Things just don't get better
than that, do they?

DADDY HART
No they don't! You can't beat that.
Nothing can beat that, ever.
The rug begins to move away towards the city houses.
TV ANCHOR WOMAN
We just caught a spectacular event.
A cute couple on a flying carpet
arrived to see the new born baby
elephant. It is a miracle! A

miracle and we have it on tape,
here tonight. I can't believe it.

The bay elephant rises and snuggles the mother. Several grownup elephants rise up on their back legs and raise up their trucks to salute the flying rug above.

Rom and Jenny wave down at them.

The rug moves away now toward the houses on the other side of the park where brother Tommy and his girl friend are sitting on the porch watching the TV coverage of the park.

Next, the rug hovers above the ranch house with Tommy and Katie.

Tommy's jaw is open wide when he spots his older sister standing with Rom on the flying carpet.

Tommy rises, rubbing his eyes.

Katie recognizes them too and places her hand over her open mouth.

Behind him the parents have risen in the living room and they pull open the drapes wider and point into the sky.

Rom and Jenny wave down as they hover above, near by.

Tommy and the teen girl wave back up from the porch.

Tommy, Katie and the shocked parents wave up too.

The rug sparkles, then pulls up and way into the dark sky again on it's own.

INT. 7-11 STORE - NIGHT

Back in the Seven Eleven Store, Wayne is watching the Zoo event repeat coverage as shown on the TV above the counter.

The attendant is eating a pretzel while sitting on the counter by the cash register.

When he sees Rom and Jenny on the TV, he jumps down off his stool and places a foot in the mop pail.

The pail has wheels and he then slides away along the floor.

Again he falls back ward, we see his feet rise upward into the air over the counter.

Dirty water rises above the counter briefly and down on Wayne.

EXT. CITY SKYLINE – NIGHT

Rom and Jenny fly down near an apartment fire where six fire trucks are parked below.

Smoke and fire are in each window.

The firemen fight the blaze madly, vigorously.

EIGHT FIREMEN wave them away.

The rug circles the roof and the fire silently goes out.

The shocked and surprised firemen below, wave thanks as Jenny and Rom begin to fly away.

Soon the rug is out of sight.

Jenny and Rom hug and kiss as the rug circles the University next.

Dr. Ballard and wife are on the steps, leaving.

Dr. Ballard looks at his pipe, then he waves slowly.

His wife hugs his arm, then, they both wave vigorously.

Rom and Jenny point away and up and the rug moves skyward.

It fly's over the river and then out toward the skyline.

It circles the EMPIRE STATE building (ANY FAMOUS BUILDING) It then heads for the Statue of Liberty (OR OTHER FAMOUS STATUE).

The rug circles the Statue of Liberty and then heads back to the suburbs. (OF NEW JERSEY OR LONG ISLAND OR SOME OTHER CITY WHERE-EVER FILMED)

A TOUR BOAT OF PEOPLE wave upward and ROM and Jenny wave back down. (MANHATTAN TOUR BOAT OR A RIVER PADDLE BOAT)

A POLICE HELICOPTER PILOT heads towards Rom and Jenny.

He hovers, scratches his head, then smiles and waves, then pulls helicopter away.

TWO CELEBRITIES (OR THREE, OR FOUR) are in the back seat of the copter pointing and laughing to each other.

All are eating burgers, fries and are holding cups of soda!
(TRAILER CLIPS - AD PLUG SET UP RIGHT HERE!)

Rom and Jenny hug and wave back.

The rug heads down over the stadium and circles the field.

The stadium crowd stops along with the players (BASEBALL OR FOOTBALL) and all goes silent for a minutes.

Rom and Jenny slowly glide thirty feet above the field as the frozen spectators silently watch.

Not a sound or a body movement is made as the crowd holds its breath.

When the rug reaches the other side it circles back again as if showing Rom and Jenny to the world. [It is like the rug is showing the world for the moment that these two are true lovers.]

The rug moves skyward and the crowd snaps into a cheerful roar of pleasure.

Applause follows, then the game resumes.

The rug disappears into the dark night, glowing magically as it moves across the star lit sky.

Rom spots a dog stuck on the top of a roof in the distance.
    The rug moves to where he points.
    Jenny points to the open window and a cat sitting near bye in a tree.

The dog jumps onto the rug and it lowers to the ground. The dog jumps off and runs up onto the front porch.

Rom hugs Jenny and the rug rises and takes off skyward.

A flash of light is seen in the sky. A balloonist has been night gliding and his balloon is losing air, the seam is ripping open.

The rug flies up next to the balloon and it descends. The man and women jump over onto the carpet and it lowers them onto a field.

The balloon crashes near by. The two take a deep breath. They smile at each other silently, half stunned, as Rom and Jenny rise skyward.

Down the road an emergency van is speeding to the hospital.
    A car in the other lane blows a tire and smacks into a telephone pole. The van pulls to the side and stops but a hot wire comes loose and falls on the van.

Rom and Jenny spot the crash and fly over the scene.

The emergency van driver jumps out and watches the wire spark the truck.

He grabs a tree limb and smacks the wire away, then opens the back door. Both men and patient are out cold. He goes inside and exits.

A young girl arrives on a bike.

She gets off and stands by the open rear door of the van.

She appears as flat chest-ed. Her dark hair's stringy.
    DRIVER
    My cell phone is out. They are
    all dead inside. Stand away
    from their little boy.
    LITTLE GIRL
    I'm a girl, not a boy. Hey.
    I see a cell phone inside.
    She jumps inside the emergency van. The man is not looking.

He looks up just when the rug flies over the vehicle. It sparkles. He steps back.
    The two aids come out, then the patient. They are all alive.
    DRIVER
    You're all alive. You were all
    dead. He had a massive heart

    attack. I felt you pulse.

    PATIENT
    (Pounding chest, smiling)
    Well I'm alright now. I feel
    like a million.

The driver scratches his head.

The little flat chest-ed girl exits the van. Her hair is golden and nicely formed. She looks up at the hovering rug in the sky and then down at her chest. She has nice boobs now. She grabs her boobs, looks up and smiles.

Rom and Jenny waves and the people below wave back. The magic carpet moves up and away.

Next the carpet heads across the water and circles about.

Below two teenagers are night riding a speedboat and drinking beer. It side swipes a red blinking buoy and tears a hole in its side.

The boat begins to slow down and takes on water.

The rug flies next to the boat, the boys hop on just before it sinks.

The rugs swiftly moves over to the docks and the boys jump off, half scared at everything. They stand and watch the speedboat go under.

Rom and Jenny shake their heads as they move up into the sky.

They fly up and back towards the city. We see a night window cleaning crew working twenty stories above the street.

Suddenly a rope breaks and a man is seen hanging by one arm from a scaffold. Jenny tugs Rom's arm and points to the man in the distance. The rug follows her command and ruches up under the man. He falls onto the rug, places both hands over his face.

The carpet lowers to the street. He sits up and then climbs off. A taxicab man parked at the curb rubs his eyes as he watches the man jump down to the sidewalk.

Rom and Jenny wave a good bye and the rug rises up again into the start lit sky.

The rug moves out of the city and flies over an Indian gabling Casino. It slows down. It travels along the glass roof. Rom and Jenny look down at the people gambling inside.

INT. CASINO – NIGHT

(Inside) We See every machine pay out at the joy of all the customers inside. The roulette wheel stops on seven and a man wins a big stack of cash. A man betting on a horse race sees the Number Eleven on the screen and jumps for joy, holding his winning ticket.

EXT. SKYLINE – NIGHT

The rug moves upward and back toward the roof top apartment.

Rom and Jenny laugh as they watch the joy break out below.

The sun is beginning to rise. The carpet circles a flock of black birds. They sparkle and then turn into a flock of white doves.

Heading towards the jail, a truck is stopped with two flat rear tires. The driver rubs his forehead as he finishes a close inspection of them. He watches the rug drop down and stands back, startled for a moment until he sees Rom and Jenny.

The rug descends and hovers over the truck and the big tires fill up with air.

The driver waves up in gratitude as the rugs moves skyward. Rom and Jenny wave back down.

The rug passes over the jail.

INT. PRISON – NIGHT

Inside a guard is knocked out and onto the floor. The inmate pulls a lever and all the cell doors open.

We hear a loud cheer from the inmates.

After the rugs passes overhead, the doors lock closed and tight. The one inmate hits the switch but they stay closed.

We hear loud grumbling.

The guard stands up and handcuffs the inmate.

The carpet flies away into the sky towards the rising sun.

Rom points toward the apartment house but Jenny points into the sky. A small two-engine plane is in trouble. Both engines are smoking badly. The plane starts descending over the city.

The runway is far away.

Both Rom and Jenny point at the plane. With unbelievable speed, faster than ever before, the rug flies out over

the plane.

Inside, through the windows, the pilots are panicking.

They spot the flying carpet and rub their eyes.

When it moves up over them, the plane rises out of it's descent. The pilots smile at each other and shrug their shoulders.

The co-pilot rugs sweat off his forehead and smiles.

PILOT

The engines are both out.
>I don't know who they are,
>but I love them, lots.
>After a short while, the plane lands safely on the runway.

The carpet pulls upward.

Rom and Jenny give a final wave to the pilots.

They pilots and passengers, wave back.

The rug disappears into the night sky.
>Next, the rug passes by the hospital.
>We see a young man being wheeled out in a wheelchair by his wife. He has a face full of stitches over his cheeks and along his neck. His hands are bandaged. (Angle On)
>He looks up at his wife. His hands and face shake as he talks.

YOUNG MAN

I'm lucky the glass didn't

> cut an artery. I'll be badly
> scared for life, honey. My
> face hurts so bad and my hands
> were almost crushed to pieces.

YOUNG WIFE

I'm just glad your alive from
the crash. The kids need you
as much as I do. Oh look up
in the sky. It's beautiful.
I must be dreaming.

The carpet slows down and hovers a moment, then circles the couple.
  Sparkles drop down and surround the couple, then, they diminish followed by snowflakes.
  The man stands up. He pulls off the bandages. He rubs his face. His face is smooth and his hands are cured.
  The wife hugs him tight. He hugs her tight. (Angle On)
  The couple wave up and Rom with Jenny wave back.
  Away they move out of sight towards the sunrise.
  We see Rom point to his watch. They pass over the Amusement Park. The rug flies over to the Ferris wheel. Rom
looks at Jenny and she at him.
  They look puzzled. Rom points down to two children.
  It has been stuck for six hours. There's a boy and girl
stuck on the top seat of the wheel. They're holding their crotches hard, waiting to get down and go to the bathroom.
  Rom points this out to Jenny. (Points to his crotch and at them)
  The rug pulls up next to the ten year old children.
  Rom and Jenny help them step on board and the rug lowers them next to the rest rooms.

The two jump down and dash to the Men's and Ladies room.

The crowd applauds. Rom and Jenny point upward and fly away.

The exhausted and relieved parents sit down on a park bench and cry on each other's shoulder.

Rom and Jenny realize that the predicament has ended so the rug takes them home. Rom and Jenny point homeward.

EXT. APARTMENT ALLEY - NIGHT
  We see the police cars pull away with all the Hoods cuffed and placed inside each car.
  The landlord waves to the offices as they leave.
  The landlord places his monkey down on his station wagon.

He looks up and sees Rom and Jenny arrive back on the roof and smiles. A stray dog walks near and growls at the cat.

The alley cat walks up next to the landlord for protection.

He watches the flying carpet pass above and move over towards the rooftop.

The landlord looks back down at the dog with fright. He then sees that the dog and cat are rubbing up together.

Mr. Pitt smiles at both animals and winks upward toward Rom and Jenny.

He bows down and pats the cat's little furry head and the dogs.

The cat responds with a purr and meow.

EXT. APARTMENTHOUSE ROOF - NIGHT

The rug slowly lowers to the roof. It hovers a few seconds, then settles down in place. The miracle ride is over.

Rom looks deeply into Jenny's eyes.

ROM

I'm so happy that you're

   alright my love.

Jenny holds Rom tight about the waist.

JENNY

Can we go up and fly around

   again?

Rom looks up into the stars, then back at Jenny.

Both look at each other now. A rainbow rises over their shoulders.

ROM

Well! Remember, my grandfather

   said that it could only happen
   once. Only once when true love
   was involved. I think he was
   with us up there tonight. We
   helped a lot of nice people.

Rom feels the envelope stuck to Jenny's blouse. He carefully pulls it out.

ROM

What's this? A letter for you?

Jenny takes the letter and looks closely at it. She tears the envelope open. She then reads it to Rom.

He stands with hands on hips calmly waiting, listening.

JENNY

It's from the University. It

says I got the job. I got the
teaching job. I'm a History
Professor. And all because

of you Rom love. I love you

so much.

Jenny kisses Rom and hugs him tight. Her hands run down his back, she feels a letter in his back pocket. Jenny pulls out the letter.
Rom looks surprised.
ROM
Oh I know. It's just a silly

letter addressed to me. I
forgot to open it up. Here.
Here, let's see it now, Jen.

It's probably a silly bill.
Silly stuff for sure.
Rom takes a big gulp of air and looks up into the stars.
Jenny looks up now too. She wonders what he's doing.
ROM
Thanks Grandpa, thank you!
JENNY
Is it from you Grandpa?
Rom smiles and kisses Jenny on the hands.
She beams and begins to blush at his excitement.
ROM
No it a wonderful blessing, Jen.
Last week I typed some numbers
in on a few lottery tickets for
a nice man in a suit. He says
here that 7-11 won the Super-Lotto.
He's sharing his winnings with me.
Now I can buy my rug store. Now we
can get married. -—For sure.
Jenny jumps back surprised and smiles up at Rom.
JENNY
Married? Oh Rom Carpenter, I do.
I do! I do! -—For sure.
Rom and Jenny hug tightly and they kiss once more.
Rom lets go for a moment to ask Jenny something else.
ROM
Jenny. How many children do you

want to have, seven or eleven?

JENNY
Two, a boy and a girl. -—For sure.
Rom gives her a quick kiss.
ROM
Jenny. I will never deceive you
by trying to be what - I - am -

not! I was very lucky this week.
I'll never forget this wonderful
night. (pause) I've learned my
lesson, -—for sure, for sure.

Jenny hesitates. She replies with a big smile.
JENNY
Good! No more Hoods or Gangsters.

We'll build a cute house under a
rainbow in a pretty, green valley
just like your Great-Grandfather
once did and make love on the rug.

Rom and Jenny embrace together and then kiss. The carpet glows bright for a moment, rising up five feet and then falling back down slowly onto the roof.

Rom and Jenny stop kissing. They look left and right. They up and look down. But, they only see the apartment roof. The floodlights flick on and then off, the dawn has broken.

They couple look skyward and watch a flock of white doves descend and circle them on the roof. (Angle on their astonished faces)

Rom and Jenny kiss again.

We pull back above the roof and we view the morning sun rising under a rainbow.

Sparkles surround the edges of the rug and roof as the young lovers embrace.

THE END

****

(1) PULL BACK OFF ROOF TOP TO A SCENIC CITY VIEW.
(2) ROLL BACK TO STARS IN TYE MORNING SKY. BEGIN
THE 7-11 THEME SONG.)
(3) BEGIN THE FILM CREDITS ROLLING OVER SMALL,
CARTOON COLORED FLYING CARPETS.

****